OSCAR OF THE *BISMARCK*

Frances Y. Evan

First Published in 2022 by Blossom Spring Publishing
Oscar Of The Bismarck © 2022 Frances Y. Evan
ISBN 978-1-7392326-2-7
E: admin@blossomspringpublishing.com
W: www.blossomspringpublishing.com
This work is based on true life events, although sometimes
enhanced by the author's imagination.
In some cases, the names of people and places have been
changed to protect the privacy of others.

INTRODUCTION

At the time of this story Germany and Britain are at war. The majority of the European continent has been defeated and is under German control. Britain and its Commonwealth stand alone. Germany now seeks to dominate the seas.

Although the United States has not yet formally entered the war, it is supporting Britain with steady shipments of supplies, food and war material. Convoys of American ships carry these supplies across the Atlantic at increasing risk and peril. Germany's intent is to sever this supply line with submarines and surface raiders.

CHAPTER ONE

OSCAR, *BISMARCK* AND THE RAT

Cats are curious, they say. I will admit that I have my fill of curiosity. I am also rather an adventurous cat. A bit of excitement and daring quite appeals to me. However, what I have lived through was above and beyond what I bargained for, and more than any cat should be expected to endure.

It began for me in 1939, February 14, 1939, to be exact. It was the day they launched the ship. They had been building it for almost three years and I had been watching. I often wandered around the shipyard dodging trucks, equipment and heavy boots to watch the buzz of activity. On a nice day, I looked for a coil of rope to curl up in where I would be mostly hidden and protected. There, I washed myself at my leisure and sometimes dozed while the great ship took shape. It was massive! The workers themselves were amazed as it grew. They stood in awe at times laughing and boasting. "Such a ship the world has never seen," they would say. "How big!" "How powerful!"

I watched on that cold winter day when the ship was launched. Thousands of people were there cheering and waving flags. All those flags frightened me. I did not like them. They were a bold shade of red with an odd, twisted cross of black. I watched from much further away than usual and saw the huge keel slide into the water as sailors in uniform lined the perimeter of the ship with their right arm outstretched stiffly in front of them. I knew it was a very big day for the people and that the ship had been built for adventure and daring on the sea. I learned the ship's name. I heard it shouted repeatedly...loudly...gloriously. Bismarck! Bismarck! **Bismarck!**

***

A handsome male cat picked its way delicately along the pier at the Blohm & Voss Shipyard in Hamburg. It flinched but was undaunted by loud clashes of metal upon metal or the sudden eruption of motorized power equipment. Gracefully it veered out of the path of vehicles and workmen as it made its way down to Dock 6. The cat walked half the length of the long hull and then jumped effortlessly atop a large wooden crate that had been stamped and labeled and awaited loading. It stretched, yawned and set about the business of washing its paws which were dusty and speckled with sawdust. The short black fur of the animal gleamed in the sun and covered the cat completely except for its muzzle and neck. There the fur was completely white. Only when it was satisfied that the paws were quite clean, did the cat look around at the activities on the dock. It was careful to display a bored, nonchalant attitude while actually it was most interested in the work in progress aboard the enormous vessel. It had been over a year now since the great ship had slowly descended the slipway into the sea and been guided by tugs to its fitting dock. The ship was meant for great things, the animal knew, because of its enormous size and the powerful-looking parts being added daily. It became mightier and more and more intimidating as it grew, looming higher and higher and casting a longer, darker shadow.

A crane loomed into the sky not far from where the cat sat in the sun. It slowly swung over the deck lowering a crate to a group of men waiting to receive it. The hook was removed and one of the men gave a shout and a wave. As the crane swung back toward the dock a worker approached the crate where the cat sat. "Sorry, Oscar," he said in an amused German voice, "We need this crate next." The cat did not stir. It knew a good number of German words and phrases and those it did not know, it could surmise from the tone and volume of the voice as well as the attitude of the speaker. He heard his name spoken with no urgency or irritation and he knew the worker well, his name was Johan. Johan was fond of Oscar, as were most of the dockworkers and he often took a couple of minutes out of his day to pet the cat. He would smooth Oscar's coat from his ears to the end of his tail and scratch gently under his chin while chatting pleasantly, complimenting him on his soft fur and good looks. Oscar waited for his usual petting but today Johan was busy. "Come on Oscar. You must get down now," he said with a little more authority in his voice. Oscar saw that Johan was looking at him expectantly and as the hook of the crane swung closer to them, he understood. The cat crouched in a stretch, both front legs extended stiffly in front. He yawned leisurely, scratched with a back paw behind one ear, and then finally, gracefully leaped down. "Good kitty," Johan praised with a brief smile as Oscar sauntered several yards away and then turned to watch the descending hook. The cat was slightly annoyed. He flicked his tail rather put out that he had been dismissed without so much as a quick stroke or pat on the head. He sat in the shadows to pout a while and watch his crate lifted off of the dock.

And then he saw it. At first it was just a familiar movement in the periphery of the cat's vision. When the cat snapped its head around, it saw the gray rat darting out from under a canvas sack. Its little feet carried it swiftly along the length of a wooden plank before it disappeared behind a stack of barrels. Oscar jumped to his feet and meowed once with irritation. It was *that* rat again, the gray rat with the little black ears that had been eluding him for weeks now. He ran quickly to the barrels keeping his eyes fixed on the spot where the rat had disappeared from view. He hunched down poking his nose into the gaps and spaces between the barrels, sniffing, listening and staring into the darkness. He thought he heard a tiny scratching sound and so waited, still as a stone, for the rodent to reappear. Oscar waited for a long time, watching intently for any movement, ready to pounce and grab and bury his paws into the soft flesh of the small creature. This rat maddened him. It would appear only for a few seconds and then scamper into a tiny hole or crevice reappearing in a different spot some time later. It seemed to be unaware or bothered by the attention of the cat, which Oscar knew could not be true because it dashed and darted and hid itself so cleverly. He felt taunted by the rat and outsmarted.

I hate that rat! It has outwitted me again! I don't think it is there anymore. It has scurried away. Probably that was the brief scratching sound that I heard a while ago. It has moved away and is laughing at me somewhere close by as I continue to wait here, hunched down, ready to pounce. I don't want to leave yet, though...just in case. I really want to catch that rat. If he just pokes his nose out for a second, I'll be on him. What a satisfying victory that will be! I'll wait a while longer. I hate that rat!

CHAPTER TWO

STEFFAN'S ARRIVAL

Oscar had found a sunny spot and a cardboard box which had been tossed away carelessly and ended up on its side. It was the perfect place to curl up for a mid-afternoon nap. No one had bothered him, so he slept deeply for a good long time. Upon waking, he noticed immediately that he was hungry and, after stretching his limbs, set out on a prowl. Usually, if he made himself highly visible strolling about the dock, some of the dock workers would offer him tidbits from their tins and bags. At dusk the cat would make its way to the squat little house nearby, south of the shipyard, where it had been brought as a kitten for the boy named Rolf. When Rolf was not at school, reading his books, riding his bicycle, or chasing a ball with his friends, he would fill Oscar's water bowl and put down a plate of scraps for him to eat. He was a kind enough boy but had outgrown his need for the companionship of a pet and did not bother with the cat very much anymore. The rest of the family, an older sister, a mother and a tired, overworked father, almost completely ignored Oscar although they did allow him to sleep on a rug in the kitchen at night.

The weather had warmed up considerably in the months since the launching and was perfect for outside dining. Oscar strolled along the dock looking for friendly dock workers, especially those sitting with open tins or bags on their laps. He sniffed the air hoping to detect tantalizing smells of fish or meat, ham or sausage. Two men sat talking quietly as they ate steadily from their lunch tins. The cat wound its body around and through their legs to get their notice. They smiled at him but apparently had nothing that day to share. "Sorry Oscar," one man said.

"Try your luck somewhere else."

"Here Puss," a friendly voice called. Oscar turned toward the voice. A group of men in dark uniforms carrying heavy, canvas bags slung over their shoulders stood in a small group. Lately the cat had noticed these new arrivals to the docks. They would stand together gazing at the ship in amazement and admiration, gesturing grandly, laughing and slapping each other on the back. "Here Puss," the voice repeated. One of the group, a very young man, squatted down and extended his arm toward the cat. Oscar waited a moment studying the gentle expression on the sailor's face and the beckoning fingers that seemed eager to touch and scratch and stroke. Nonchalantly and unhurriedly, he strode toward the seaman. He touched his nose to the outstretched fingers and then stepped closer. The hands of the young man were large and rough and petted him vigorously. He stroked firmly the whole length of the cat from the crown of his head to the end of his tail and scratched under Oscar's chin with both hands. Oscar rubbed his body against the man's knees and arms turning in circles so that every part of him could feel the affectionate touch of the young man.

The dock worker, who had not had any offerings for Oscar, watched with amusement and called out to the seaman, "Oscar, his name is Oscar. He's always hanging around the docks. Makes a bit of a pest of himself sometimes." The young man looked up, nodded at the dock worker and turned his attention back to Oscar.

"Oscar, is it? Hello Oscar. My name is Steffan. What a nice boy you are, so handsome…so sleek." He continued his petting and stroking while the other sailors in his group looked on grinning, chuckling and nudging each other. Steffan looked up briefly and grinned back at them. "I had a cat as a boy, Mina was her name. I had her since she was a kitten. She died only recently. I like cats." He turned back to Oscar and swung the heavy canvas bag off of his shoulder. "Let's see if I have anything in here for you, Oscar." He furrowed down to the deepest depths of the bag until he felt the rustle of paper and then withdrew a bulging paper bag. "You're a hungry kitty, aren't you? Do you like liverwurst Oscar?" Steffan tore a piece of liverwurst from a roll in the bag and held it out to the cat. Oscar stretched his neck forward until his nose was almost touching it. He sniffed for a few moments and licked it once before taking the liverwurst into his mouth. After swallowing, his little pink tongue darted in and out cleaning the fur around his mouth as he looked expectantly at Steffan.

"Ah so you liked it, did you?" Steffan chuckled. "Want some more? He tore off a bigger piece and placed it on the ground in front of the cat. Oscar hunched down and ate contentedly while the young man looked on smiling.

I made a new friend today. He told me that his name is

Steffan. I could tell he liked me because his voice was kind, and his touch was firm but gentle. He gave me something to eat from his bag that tasted very good. The other young men in his group thought it was funny that he took a little time with me. But Steffan did not seem to mind, and he stayed hunched down talking to me and petting me while they continued their conversation and moved along down the dock.

They all belong to the ship. I think that the ship is nearly ready to leave, and the young men will go too in their dark uniforms with their big bags. I know this because I have been around the docks for a long time, and I watch and learn.

CHAPTER THREE

OSCAR ABOARD

Oscar watched for his friend during the next few months. Steffan spent a lot of time aboard the great ship but did leave for a day or two every once in a while with a group of sailors. They would stroll along the dock talking animatedly and laughing. If Steffan spotted Oscar, he stopped to scratch him under his neck and promised to bring him a treat when he returned. A couple of sailors pulled out cigarettes and lit up while they waited for their shipmate looking on with mocking expressions. One evening Steffan returned by himself. He was whistling softly and walking a little unsteadily, veering a little wider than necessary to avoid obstacles in his path. Oscar was curled up on a discarded burlap bag but perked up his head when he heard his friend approach. He stretched and headed toward him wondering what delicious tidbit the sailor might have in his pocket when he caught a familiar flash of movement to his left. He swiveled his head sharply and saw a rat, *the rat*, dash across the dock and under a gangplank where it met the concrete surface of the wharf. Oscar switched direction in a flash, hunched down and stalked silently with his eyes glued to the spot where the rat had disappeared. Steffan noticed the cat and watched him moving stealthily along the dock, weaving smoothly around ropes, crates and equipment, low to the ground, focused…in pursuit. Then, it all happened in a flash. The rat came out from under the gangplank and scurried along the width of it tucked against the angle edge that it formed with the wharf surface. It stopped suddenly sniffing the air and sensing imminent danger. Its tiny head snapped around, saw its pursuer, turned sharply and darted up the gangplank. Without a moment's hesitation, Oscar followed, sprinting across the dock, up the gangplank and onto the great ship. Steffan felt in his pocket for the piece of fish wrapped in paper that he had saved for Oscar. He chuckled to himself. So, there was a new shipmate aboard. Well, then. "Welcome aboard, Oscar," he said to himself. "Welcome aboard *Bismarck*."

I find myself on the main deck of the great ship. Bismarck. I have heard the name repeated often and I remember when the name was shouted proudly on the day it was launched. I have chased the rat aboard Bismarck and watched it slip smoothly beneath a jumble of boxes, crates and equipment and disappear from sight. That rat has escaped me again...for now. I am determined to catch that creature. Now, I will have to hunt it aboard ship.

I look around me and I am humbled by this new world. Gray...this new world is gray and cold and hard and big and powerful. I back up on the deck and cower amongst the supplies to take it all in. I see wondrous sights; a long, wood deck stretching grandly into the distance, huge structures looming far above me, great mounted turrets and guns, poles, rails, metal ladders, hatches, cables, hoses, lifeboats.

I see Stefan come on board. I watch him swaying slightly as he walks along the deck. He stops suddenly and with a smooth, practiced movement he grasps a rail, steps over a lip around a hole in the deck and descends a steep metal ladder. I watch his head disappear in a flash and hear the rapid clanging rhythm of his steps on the rungs. I stare at the hole wondering if I should follow my friend. Surely Steffan has a treat for me. He always brings something back from town. However, that hole that disappears below the deck into the bowels of the ship looks ominous. I should be cautious. Perhaps I should…tiny movement at the corner of my vision. Rat. It's that rat. It's headed for the hole. I'm up and running, chasing. It's running down the handrail. I'm right behind, over the lip and trotting down the rungs. Cannot let it get away. Must catch it. I hate that rat!

***

Life aboard *Bismarck* was very different for Oscar from his life on the docks. Below the main deck the great ship was compartmentalized. There was a designated space for every necessary activity. When it was busy and sailors were hurrying to and fro, Oscar lay low. He found a spot out of the way, out of the path of the crew, and watched. When things were quieter, especially in the evening, he wandered around investigating as unobtrusively as possible.

It was on one of these scouting missions a few days after coming aboard that the cat came upon his friend, Steffan. Crew members were clearing the wardroom, a large space where they had been eating. They were folding up tables and benches. Steffan caught sight of

Oscar as he turned from the chair rack. "Oscar!" he called. "Well, it's about time. I've been watching for you. Where have you been hiding, puss? Where have you been hiding?" Steffan squatted down, stretched out his arm and snapped his fingers repeatedly. The cat trotted eagerly over to his friend and accepted his attentions. He rubbed and nuzzled and purred as Steffan stroked and scratched. "Good timing, Oscar," he said. "We've just finished chow. Hey fellas," he called to the other sailors who were working in the room.

"Any scraps left on those trays for old Oscar here?" Heads turned and young sailors halted their work for a moment to gaze at the unexpected appearance of a cat in their midst. A few approached and extended a hand to gently squeeze or pat or stroke. Others gathered up scraps and leavings from a pile of trays and made a reasonably appealing, assorted offering. Karl, of the gunnery crew, placed a plate on the floor before Oscar and the young men watched to see if the food would be acceptable. The cat sniffed and licked and then sat to eat leisurely. Karl looked on smiling. "Sehr gut, Oscar," he said. "Eat up. There is work for you too aboard Bismarck."

"Indeed, there is," Steffan added. "I'll take him around

and introduce him to the galley crew. I'm sure they will be pleased to have Oscar on duty." He stroked the cat's sleek back as he ate and the men drifted back to their chores, sweeping, mopping and stacking.

"Are you a good hunter, Oscar?" Steffan asked quietly. "Think you can catch a mouse or two for us?" He chuckled. "Nice to have you aboard, Puss. Nice to have you aboard."

Can I catch a mouse or two? I almost choked on a piece of meat. Can I catch a mouse or two? What did he think I had been doing all those months on the docks? I am an expert hunter. I'll clear Bismarck of mice and rats...no problem. I will consider that my job, my duty aboard this ship. I will earn my keep and the companionship and gratitude of Steffan and these young men. I will also make it my business to hunt down that rat, the one with the little black ears. I will find it, outsmart it, catch it and kill it. Then I will honor my friend, Steffan and lay it at his feet. I will be victorious. I will be supreme. I will win. I will prove myself worthy of this mighty ship.

***

Oscar spent evenings and nights in the wardroom with Steffan and the many other seamen who ate, slept and passed their off-duty time there. After the evening meal, the room was cleaned, cleared of tables and benches and hammocks were slung from their hooks. Steffan lifted Oscar into his hammock where he would stretch, yawn and settle down for the night. He drifted off to sleep to the sound of young voices engaged in all kinds of conversations. Sometimes the voices were raised in argument when the seamen touched on war strategies or politics, sometimes voices erupted in laughter when they joked or made fun of each other and sometimes it was quieter as men drifted off to sleep and voices were lowered playing cards or talking of family and home. When Steffan joined him in the hammock Oscar settled comfortably alongside, snug against the warmth of his body, purring contentedly.

The day after Oscar's arrival in the wardroom, Steffan took him on a limited tour of the great battleship. He carried the cat easily in one arm so that the other was free to grasp ladders, door handles and railings. He proceeded aft from the wardroom and down several deck levels. Oscar took note of the route realizing quickly that he was being shown relevant spaces aboard ship where he was meant to go. Steffan had recently finished his shift in the engine room and the cat's sensitive nose detected the smell of grease, chemicals and sweat.

The first destination was to the seaman's pantry. Several men were on duty there organizing sacks and bins and counting the stores. Steffan nodded to them as he bent to place Oscar on the floor. "I'm showing Oscar his territory," he explained looking around. "I'll let him sniff around a bit…expect he can be quite useful down here."

"Ja," affirmed Matrose-Gefreiter Conrad Rudeck, a young red-headed seaman with an easy smile. "We'd be grateful if he would catch the varmints that did that!" He inclined his head toward a sack of potatoes on the floor. The burlap bag had been gnawed through and several potatoes were scattered about half eaten and turning brown. "They have managed to get into our cold storage too and eaten chunks out of vegetables, fruit and cheese."

"Hear that, Oscar? You can really help out down here."

The cat was already checking the place out. He had his nose to the floor and followed the scent trails of little creatures. He headed to the burlap bag on the floor sniffing all around it, poking his nose inside for a while. He walked the complete perimeter of the room, checking behind bins and barrels and looking into dark corners while the crewmen looked on approvingly.

I understand what Steffan and the crew expect of me. They want me to rid them of the mice and rats aboard the ship. Little feet and gnawing teeth have contaminated some of the food stores. I can sense them all around this storage room. I will catch them. I will hide here and surprise them. I am stronger than they and smarter. They cannot escape me. I am a great hunter.

***

Steffan scooped up his feline friend and continued on with the tour. Next stop was the forward galley. There was a lot of activity there as the galley crew prepared for the evening meal. There were men chopping, stirring, measuring, carrying pots, plates and utensils, mopping, scrubbing and wiping. Steam rose above large cauldrons set atop huge stoves. A wholesome meaty aroma filled the air mingling with the unmistakable smell of freshly baked bread. There were rows of shallow pans lined up on tables near the ovens ready to be baked. Looked like some kind of apple crumb dessert to Steffan whose mouth began to water expectantly.

A large, burly crewman, the chief cook, strode purposefully toward Steffan complaining loudly, "Nein, nein Matrosen-Obergefreiter. Leave now. I do not need you getting in the way." And then he noticed Oscar. "Ah, but you have a miezekatze. What a nice puss." His tone of voice changed completely becoming high pitched and childlike as he scratched the cat on top of his head. "His name is Oscar," said Steffan. "I'm showing him places where he can be useful."

"Ah, Oscar, is it? Well, Oscar I am Oberfahnrich zur See Otto. You come and see me anytime. I've got treats for a nice miezakatze and you can keep all the nasty mice away. What a nice puss you are, Oscar. What a pretty puss."

The men in the kitchen had all stopped their work and were watching the tender scene. They had various expressions of amusement on their faces, crooked smiles and broad grins as they shot side glances at each other in shared jest. Aware of the inactivity behind him, chief cook Otto glanced around. "Alright you scoundrels, you've had your fun. Now get on with it." He gave the cat another quick rub and squeeze before turning back to his duties. "Come back and see me later, Oscar. I'll have some tasty scraps for you."

I like Lieutenant Otto. I shall go back to his kitchen very soon.

***

Steffan took Oscar to the NCO mess on the upper deck, a couple of potato storage rooms, the bakery, the forward canteens, more pantries and all the way down to the cold storage rooms. The cat paid careful attention along the route, noting the sights, sounds and smells of different areas so that he would be able to find his way later by himself. He tried not to be too distracted by the many young seamen who stared in delighted surprise or who approached to inquire about his presence on the ship, or who reached out to touch his fur.

Finally, they ended up on the main deck astern. It was a glorious evening. The air was warm and clear. The sun was in its descent, but it would be several hours until sunset. Steffan moved to the rail and leaned against it looking out over the water. He absentmindedly stroked the top of Oscar's head lightly with the tips of his fingers as he allowed his thoughts to wander. He thought of Heidelberg, his home and of his dear mother, Anna who cared so lovingly for her family, of his father, Albert, busy creating wonders in his woodshop, and of his younger sister, Trina who was so full of life and laughter. He thought of his childhood friends, all grown men now, scattered and serving the Fatherland in the air, on land and upon the sea. He was proud of the years he had spent serving in the Kriegsmarine and was excited about what lay ahead for him aboard this magnificent battleship. What great luck to be assigned to the mighty *Bismarck*!

In the weeks since Steffan took me about, I have come to know the battleship quite well…at least the areas where I have responsibilities. I have found every pantry, kitchen, canteen, storeroom and wardroom. I am welcome in all of these places. The seamen are always happy to see me, and they let me wander around wherever I want to go. They appreciate my work and praise me when they find my little dead offerings on the floor. I have caught seventeen mice and two rats so far. Not too shabby!

I saw that rat with the little black ears a few days ago. I saw it dart across the passageway and into a pantry on a lower deck. The door was ajar, and a couple of seamen were working in there. They had not seen the rat, but they noticed me. "Hello there, katze," one of them said over his shoulder as he lifted a box from an upper shelf. "Making your rounds?" I poked around sniffing and listening, watching for a sudden movement or flick of a tail. After a while I laid down in a corner to wait, out of the way of the seamen's' feet. I waited expectantly, ready to lunge at the slightest movement. It was here. I had it cornered. But I waited in vain. The rat did not appear again. When the crewmen were finished one of them held the door open for me. "Come on katzchen," he said. "We are all done here. Got to lock up now." I stood up slowly and sauntered to the door. Looking back over my shoulder I gave a short, sharp meow to voice my frustration and then left.

CHAPTER FOUR

KOMMANDANT LINDEMANN

Battleship *Bismarck* was nearing completion during the summer of 1940 as more and more of the crew arrived, took up their posts and became familiar with the ship. In the evenings, crewmen who had no watch were permitted to go on leave into Hamburg. Oscar watched them come and go and could have trotted down the gangplank anytime for a stroll onshore or perhaps a visit with his dockworker friends, but he decided to stay aboard ship. He had all the company, food and comfort that he needed, and he took his mouse-catching duties very seriously. Oscar's reputation had spread about the ship, and he had been "borrowed" for a day to patrol the officer's wardroom on the upper deck where a persistent mouse had been observed several times spoiling the officers' appetites. It had been easy to catch. Oscar had hidden in a shadowy corner after the evening meal and waited for the mouse to appear. He saw it scurrying along a wall, its nose twitching, looking for crumbs and tiny morsels of food dropped from plates and tables during dinner. The cat watched the little creature as the familiar excitement and anticipation grew. The squat, fat little body on its nimble tiny legs, the pink feet, pointed little face, shining black eyes and long sleek tail, never failed to enthrall him and spark his natural instinct to catch, hold, mall and completely dominate. Oscar tensed, held perfectly still as the mouse drew nearer, and then he attacked. He pounced catching the animal between his front paws and then grasping it by the neck with his sharp, pointed teeth. The soft flesh yielded, and the little mouse was dead in an instant. The cat carried its prey to the middle of the room and placed on the floor so that it would be easily seen by the crewman who next entered the wardroom. He sat for a while beside his conquest cleaning himself. He licked his paws and washed his face, ears and whiskers. With his back leg he gave himself a vigorous scratch under the neck before rising and casually sauntering out of the room when the door was next opened and headed back to his rounds below decks.

Later that day when he wandered into the central kitchen, chief cook Otto greeted him warmly. "Ach, Oscar. Here you are. I have been saving a special treat for you." He hurried to a counter beside a stovetop where a huge cauldron steamed and picked up a plate. "No scraps tonight, Oscar, I cooked up a little fresh fish just for you. I poached it so it should be nice and tender." Otto set the plate on the floor and watched with satisfaction as the cat approached, sniffed and settled down to eat heartily. He chuckled to himself. "Good job today my clever miezekatze. I heard that the officers were singing your praises when they saw that you had caught that mouse in their wardroom."

"Sehr gut, Oscar," a kitchen worker called over his shoulder as he passed by carrying a stack of trays. "Ach, listen he is purring," Otto said to the young man's retreating back. "Do you hear that? He is purring. Are you happy then my miezekatze?" He said addressing Oscar again and bending down to gently caress the top of the cat's head between his ears. "Yes, you are, aren't you? You are happy with your tasty fish and you're happy here with us aboard Bismarck." Chief cook Otto passed a pleasant minute more chatting with his furry friend before sighing, standing and surveying his kitchen. "Ach, nein, Matrose Schmidt, do not take from that pot. I have not checked it yet." And he strode off to supervise his kitchen staff.

Mmmmm! Delicious. Did I mention that I like chief cook Otto? He is a kind and caring man. He gently stroked my head while I ate. I even stopped eating for a moment to nuzzle his hand quickly in thanks. I think he admires my "mouser" prowess. It is nice to be appreciated. It's good to be the cat!

***

Late in August a special ceremony took place aboard *Bismarck*. The great battleship was formally commissioned and joined the Kriegsmarine. Puzzled by the absence of crewmen below decks and lured by the activity on the main deck, Oscar headed topside. It was a disappointing day for August. The air was cool, a stiff wind blew and there was not the least hint of sunshine. The entire crew of 2,065 men was assembled on deck preparing to participate in the formalities. Oscar climbed a series of ladders on the superstructure of the ship to be out of the way and high enough to observe the proceedings. He found a spot by a lifeboat where he would be protected from the wind and settled down to watch.

August 24, 1940 certainly was a special day. The crew

looked magnificent in their dark navy pea coats and caps standing in straight, neat rows of three and four on both sides of the upper deck. Officers wore silver-brocade belts and their ceremonial daggers. Shiny buttons, insignias, epilates, and gold braid contrasted dramatically against dark uniforms making for a spectacular sight. The band was assembled and farther aft beneath a turret stood a group of representatives from Blohm & Voss shipbuilders. The First Officer's voice barked out commanding the crew to "Attention! Face to starboard," and the bugler sounded the alert as Kommandant Lindemann approached the battleship in a white motorboat. The honor guard presented arms and the Boson piped the Kommandant aboard. Lindemann inspected the officers, honor guard, and then reviewed the crew before stepping up to the podium on the quarterdeck. His address was impassioned and full of confidence as he asked each seaman to do his very best. He focused on the need for military might to solve the issues of the day and assured his young crew, whose average age was only twenty-one years of age that the splendid battleship, *Bismarck*, would fulfill any mission assigned to her. Then, he commanded, "Hoist flag and pennant!" The band played the national anthem as the flag was raised on the flagstaff and the pennant on the mainmast. When the wind caught them, they waved and furled briskly.

I could hear the flags snapping in the wind from my spot. I was amazed at the number of sailors on deck. I could tell that this was an important, formal ceremony and when the band played, the seamen lifted their faces to watch the flags rise above them. Their expressions were serious and resolute, and I thought I saw tears in some of their eyes. I scanned the rows finding many faces I knew including Karl, the gunner and Conrad from the pantry but I could not see Steffan or Otto. Perhaps they were further away from me and out of my view. Well, someone very important came on board. He spoke to the crew from a podium where everyone could see him. I'm guessing he is in charge of the ship. Lindemann is his name. Kommandant Lindemann. He seems to be well respected by his men. Perhaps I will meet him one day.

***

Training and exercises aboard Bismarck became more

intense and rigorous after Kommandant Lindemann arrived. The Kommandant involved himself in all aspects of the activities, checking procedures, attending training, inspecting construction and installations, asking questions, supervising work in progress, reviewing reports and issuing orders. The crew became familiar with the ship, crawling through tight and narrow spaces in the hold, locating stowage spaces and workshops, as well as climbing the bridge and towers. There were frequent alarms signaling aircraft drills, fire drills, damage-control exercises and clear-for-action exercises. The drills became more and more routine as the young crew grew more proficient and confident at their duty stations. The daily schedule was as follows:

0600	Reveille
0630	Breakfast
0715	Sweep decks and clean up
0800	Muster
	Work or instruction
1130	Noon break
1330	Work or instruction
1700	Evening meal

1830   Sweep decks and clean up

2200   Swing hammocks.

It was shortly after the evening meal one day in early September when Oscar abruptly crossed paths with Kommandant Lindemann. The cat was strolling toward the kitchen to visit chief cook Otto just as Lindemann, who had decided on an impromptu inspection, was leaving it. The captain stopped short and gazed down at Oscar in astonishment. Otto held his breath and the kitchen staff stared nervously as they observed this meeting from where they stood, still at attention, inside the kitchen doorway. Did the Kommandant like cats? What would his reaction be? Oscar sat down and waited patiently, understanding that this man held his fate in his hands. He could be tossed off the ship, banished, cast out, with just one word from him. But Lindemann's expression relaxed and softened into a smile as he bent over and smoothed the soft fur on the top of his head. "Matrose Oscar," he said. "I have heard of your skill. Keep up the good work." With a wider smile he gave a quick salute and continued on his way.

I met the great captain. It was tense there for a moment. I didn't know what to expect. I could see Otto and the others all waiting and wondering too. But the good Kommandant was gracious, spoke kindly to me and actually saluted before he left. I was so stunned that I couldn't immediately react. I wanted to salute him also. I raised a paw but the best I could manage was a scratch behind my ear. It didn't matter anyway because the Kommandant had already turned and was striding purposefully away.

I have heard Lindemann's name all over the ship. The crew thinks highly of him and speaks of him with great respect. I think he must be an honorable man and a great leader.

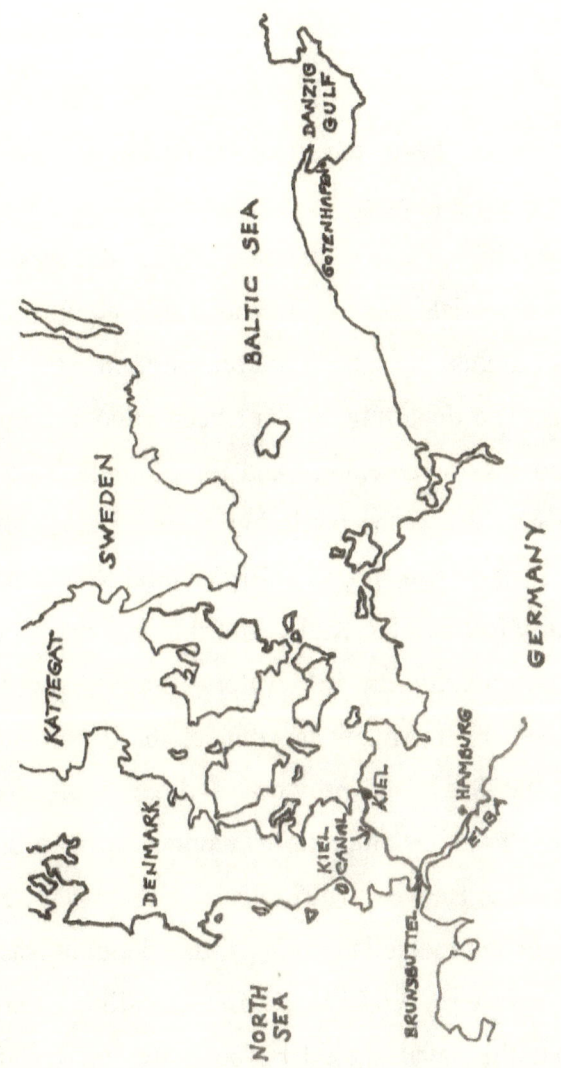

THE BALTIC SEA

CHAPTER FIVE

GUNS AND THE RAT

On September 15, 1940, the great Battleship *Bismarck* departed from the equipping pier at the Blohm and Voss Shipyard on route to the Baltic Sea. There she was to perform her sea trials, testing all the ship's equipment, navigation systems, speed, fuel consumption, and of course, guns. The departure had not been announced so there was no fuss or ceremony and no admirers waved from the riverbanks as the battleship steamed along the Elbe River. *Bismarck* anchored in Brunsbuttel Roads that evening, ready to enter the Kiel Canal the next day. The Kiel Canal was a sixty-one-mile waterway built between 1887 and 1895 by Germany to connect the North Sea with the Baltic Sea. This provided a direct route and eliminated the need for shipping to navigate around the Jutland peninsula. Between 1907 and 1914 the canal was enlarged to accommodate larger ships, dreadnought class battleships. Following World War I, the Versailles Treaty specified that the canal should be open for use by all nations but in 1936 Adolf Hitler repudiated these terms and took control.

Oscar decided to spend some time topside that first evening of the *Bismarck*'s departure. He bounded up the last metal ladder welcoming the rush of cool, fresh air as he arrived on deck. There was a small crowd; mostly officers, gathered aft and the cat strolled in that direction curious to discover what had brought them there. Suddenly a roar filled the air. Oscar jumped straight up half a foot before dashing to find cover. He squeezed behind an open hatch door and waited rather rankled at the disturbance. The ship was dropping anchor. The great chain rumbled rapidly and fiercely before stopping abruptly. The cat waited a while after the officers dispersed before he emerged from his hiding place to be sure the noise would not start up again. He was agitated as he continued his walk, annoyed at having been caught unawares and secretly embarrassed at having bolted in fright. He hoped that no one had noticed him. He did not think so since the crew on deck had been focused on the clamorous activity at the bow.

Darkness crept across the sky while Oscar found a sheltered spot out of the night breeze to sit and watch the lights of the town on shore and to enjoy a little time of solitude. Soon he would meander back down to the wardroom, after it was cleaned and swept, and the hammocks were swung. He yawned and shifted into a hunched, half laying position settling in for a while, allowing his eyes to squeeze shut for a minute or two as he dozed on and off…on and off…on and off…

I was jolted out of my drowse most jarringly! I leapt to my feet my head spinning trying to determine the source of the loud wailing. The sound was dreadful, piercing the calm night air with an ominous warning. My hair stood on end and my back arched instinctively as I anticipated danger and raced for the ladder to escape below deck. I had to back off, however, and retreat to my hiding place because crewmen were pounding up the ladder, the metallic clang of shoes on ladder rungs adding to the overall racket. The men hurtled on deck and sprinted to gun housings where they hastily sat, swiveled and took aim. They were pointing up to the sky where a light from the mainland shone into the darkness. And then the shooting began; rapid, repeating fire from several areas on the ship. I shrank down anxiously into my space very disturbed, very unhappy, and waited for this horrific episode to end.

***

When Oscar appeared in the wardroom after the air raid ended it was obvious that he was in an agitated state. He startled and tensed at any sudden sound, an outburst of laughter, the clank of a pan on a tabletop, the quick, sharp scrape of a chair leg on the deck floor. Steffan noticed his hesitant approach and swept him up in his arms to hold him close. "Ach, puss, you were not up top, were you? Ach, poor Oscar, did you get caught in the air raid?" Steffan smoothed the fur on top of Oscar's head, between his shoulder blades and down the upper part of his back. Tickling him under his neck he continued to jabber soothingly, "It's alright now puss, you're safe down here. What were you thinking…going up top? Did Otto give you your dinner? Was it tasty, Oscar? Was it a nice, tasty dinner?"

Karl looked over his shoulder from where he was hanging his hammock. "Got a bit of the taste of the war, did you Oscar?" He said with a wry smile. "Well, probably won't be your last." Steffan ignored Karl and lifted Oscar into his hammock. "I'm on watch tonight, puss, so you have the hammock all to yourself for a while. There, there," he said with a final slow, sweeping stroke along the cat's spine all the way to the end of the tail. "Relax now and go to sleep." Steffan grabbed his watch cap and jacket and hurried out of the wardroom as Oscar curled up in the hammock. He was calm now after the soothing attentions of his friend. He listened for a while to the deep voices of the young seamen speculating about the air raid and the sea trials ahead and then the chatter blended into background noise, and he drifted off to sleep.

Battleship *Bismarck* passed through the Kiel Canal the next morning, September 16th, with two tugboats guiding and assisting. There was a lot of interest on deck, but Oscar was not inclined to venture topside again so soon after the past night's events. He headed for the kitchen for some breakfast before setting out on his rounds. The kitchen was buzzing with activity as usual as the crew was cleaning up from breakfast and preparing for the noonday meal. The cat located Otto who was standing at a stovetop in front of a huge steaming cauldron. He held the lid in one hand while he stirred vigorously with the other. Oscar padded across the floor and sat at Otto's feet waiting patiently for a while before he uttered one short, sharp "meow." Chief cook Otto turned his head and looked down. "Och, my miezkatze. There you are. Just a minute now, wait a minute." He stirred the pot a little longer, turned down the heat and called to a seaman who was stacking plates. "Matrose Schmidt, watch this stew for a minute." He strode briskly over to a large refrigerator with Oscar at his heels. "Here you are my little friend," he said yanking on the fridge door and extracting a small, covered dish. "Enjoy your breakfast." Otto placed the dish on the floor and set a small bowl of water down beside it. He leaned back against the counter gazing down fondly at the cat as it chomped away hungrily. "Some critter has been getting into our sacks of oatmeal, Oscar," he said. "Perhaps you could check out that storeroom on your rounds today." The cat stopped eating briefly and looked up at the cook. "Good puss, there's a good puss, see what you can do for us, will you?" Oscar took a step toward his friend and rubbed against his legs before returning his attention back to the dish on the floor. The cook chuckled to himself, "Och, miezekatze, Oscar, sometimes I almost believe you understand everything I say to you." He pushed himself away from the counter, surveyed the kitchen and headed back to his stoves.

Chief cook Otto, but I do understand what you say. You assume that because I cannot speak, I do not comprehend. I am a clever cat, always listening and learning. I rubbed against you to let you know that I heard and accepted your request.

I left the kitchens and immediately headed for the storeroom. I know the one where the oatmeal sacks are stored, and I had to descend three decks to get there. I passed several crewmen on my way most of whom acknowledged me with a quick smile or word. Able Seaman Conrad waited for me to descend a ladder before climbing up and he actually gave me a salute when I reached the bottom. I must admit that it made me feel rather important, but I didn't have time to dally. I had my duty to perform. The storeroom door was ajar, and I slinked in noiselessly. It was dim inside. Not all the lights were on and there were indications that someone had been in the process of selecting goods for the kitchens, perhaps Conrad had been working there. I walked the perimeter of the room and inspected the sacks of oatmeal.

I realized at once why chief cook Otto had been concerned. Several sacks on a low shelf had been gnawed through and oatmeal had spilled out onto the floor. It was the work of the rat with the little black ears. I knew it right away. I jumped up onto the shelf and settled down behind the sacks, hunched down in the shadows. There was a rare quietness in the storeroom as I waited. The engines droned a low, distant thrum as the ship cruised slowly though the canal and the crew worked at a relaxed pace at their stations. I waited, still as stone, and listened. Some time passed, enough time that I began to feel drowsy, but I forced myself to stay awake. I could not fall asleep while on duty! More time passed and then a stirring caught my ear followed by a tell-tale scurrying. Tense and on instant high alert, my eyes stared wide open in the direction of the tiny sound. Flattening myself lower on the shelf I wiggled my hips in readiness for the pounce and when the little varmint appeared I lunged reflexively even as disappointment flooded through me. It was a mouse, not my black-eared rat! Trapping it beneath my paws, I squeezed the breath out of it before grasping it in my jaws to shake it back and forth vigorously. The little body was limp, but I batted it around the shelf for a while making sure it was dead before pushing it onto the floor. I slunk back into my hiding place and waited again. Time passed. I heard footsteps approach and thought it was Able Seaman Conrad returning but the footsteps moved on by and disappeared into the vastness of the great ship. I don't know how long I waited but it was long enough that I felt the pangs of hunger return and I was considering abandoning my post when I suddenly knew the rat was there. I'm not sure how I knew. I think I sensed rather than heard the little soft belly rub against the wall, and then listening intently, I detected the tiniest tick of claw against hard surface. I did not move...not a muscle as the rat moved closer and closer. And then it was on top of the sack heading toward the opening at the bottom. It stopped suddenly just as my head appeared from the shadows. For one split second we encountered each other. I saw dark eyes staring into mine, a little pink nose twitching rapidly, stiff gray whiskers and those black ears that identified it as my elusive arch enemy. I leapt in one smooth motion, pushing my body up and out, stretching my limbs to their limit and extending my claws long and wide. I felt the rat's long, sleek tail beneath one paw but even as I reached with the other to sink claws deep into the fur and skin of its back, I felt the tail slither away, sliding between my spread toes and out of my grasp. In a flash the rat darted across the sack and disappeared into the dark crevices between. I heard it scurrying away to escape through tiny seams and openings to who knows where and I cried out in frustration, a long, lamenting, agonized "meeeeeooooow."

***

After passing through the Kiel Canal, *Bismarck* was based at Gotenhafen naval base in the Baltic Sea. There she spent two months conducting tests and trials on all systems and actions aboard ship. Measured mile tests culminated in a full speed sail where the mighty ship attained a speed of 30.1 knots (35.8 mph), faster than any battleship in the British Royal Navy. Sophisticated rangefinders were installed at Gotenhafen and in mid-November *Bismarck* tested her guns at sea.

A cold, damp mist greeted Oscar when he ventured on deck early one morning. The world was dreary gray. The sea and sky blended together with no discernable horizon. The cat thought about climbing the superstructure to a lifeboat from where he could survey the ocean, the docks if they were in port, and a good portion of the ship. He could also curl up unseen and undisturbed in the boat for a long nap. However, this morning was too damp and cold for that. There had not been any warm days for a long time now, Oscar realized, and winter was fast approaching. He sat for a while just to breathe in fresh, sea air and watch the comings and goings of the crew on deck. There seemed to be more activity than usual, more sailors on duty than most mornings reporting to officers, checking clipboards, and relaying instructions. He saw his friend Karl head over to an auxiliary gun turret with some documents. A small group gathered around looking at them as Karl made wide sweeping arm motions pointing in several directions out to sea. One of the officers in the group studied Karl's papers intently, nodded and smiled broadly. Oscar had noticed this officer before. He was Kapitanleutnant Mullenheim-Rechberg, a very well-liked and respected officer aboard ship. He was a skilled artillery officer, an expert range finder and interpreter of artillery data. Karl spoke about him in glowing terms.

Below deck things also seemed out of sorts. The entire

crew was on duty it seemed, and the wardroom was vacant. The kitchen was quiet as the few seamen on duty there stopped and started their work as though waiting or anticipating something. Oscar watched the kitchen crew for a while sensing the tension in the air and wondering at the cause. He strolled over to the pantry to have a look around. A lower cabinet door was ajar, so he eased his nose inside to open it wider just as the first guns blasted up on deck.

The cat jerked around, eyes wide, shoulders hunched and tail swishing angrily from side to side. He backed into the dark cabinet and lay low listening apprehensively. The guns boomed from different areas on deck, deep, powerful explosions that rumbled and rolled like thunder throughout the ship. There were long pauses between volleys during which performance was analyzed, ranges were calculated, and calibrations were made. During one extended pause, Oscar thought that the firing was finished, and he emerged from his hiding place just as another burst rang out. He dodged back inside and sank gloomily into the shadows again waiting for the exercises to cease. In the late afternoon when firing seemed to be restricted to the lesser guns and volleys were more sporadic, the cat crept out of the cabinet and headed toward the wardroom. Passing a ladder however, Oscar hesitated and stared upward. Curiosity got the better of him and he bounded up until he reached the main deck. The sharp, acrid smell of propellant assailed his nostrils and a haze of smoke drifted astern. Oscar emerged on the port side of the battleship when a starboard side gun fired. He hunched low and made his way aft until he was clear to cross to starboard. Huddling close to the deck housing, he navigated his way until he could see the secondary guns and he waited pressed tight against a cold, steel wall. When the guns fired in a series of volleys, Oscar flinched and tucked in even more, but he marveled at the extraordinary display of power and might. He was overawed by the deafening blast of the guns as they fired and as he watched the accompanying belch of smoke, he wondered if weapons such as these, of such violence and magnitude, had ever been seen before. Mankind was indeed an ingenious species.

During the next two weeks the guns were tested at various intervals and the crew, as well as Oscar, became accustomed to the barrage from above decks. Everyone went about their usual routine without too much thought of the firing of the guns. The weather turned colder and colder as the days passed. Ice began to form in the harbor shallows and showers of snow blew in on the arctic wind. When not on his rounds, Oscar spent his time either in the steamy, warm kitchen with his friend, Otto, or in the wardroom with Steffan and the crew.

One morning after breakfast, Oscar decided to inspect the officers' wardroom. He had not heard of any more complaints since he hunted down the little mouse that had settled in there, but he thought he should pay a visit anyway. He climbed above deck and waited outside the door for someone to open it for him. It was not long before a seaman came along and noticed him there. Oscar recognized him as the artillery officer he had seen on deck on the first day of gun testing. "Ah, Oscar, you're all the way up here, are you? Did you want to check around in there?" Lieutenant Commander Mullenheim-Rechberg asked reaching out for the door handle. "There you are little one...in you go." He pushed the door open and watched the cat slide inside. "You're a good worker, Oscar, a good fellow to have around."

The officers' wardroom was vacant, so Oscar inspected slowly and thoroughly. He wove in and out of the table and chair legs then poked his nose into corners, under carts and behind cabinets. He jumped up onto a countertop and looked for signs of tiny footprints or mouse droppings. He saw nothing but decided that he would stay on watch for a while until someone came in and let him back out. The cat noticed an empty wooden box that someone had left on the seat of one of the chairs. He dropped down from the countertop, hopped up onto the chair and settled himself inside the box. It felt very good in there. The sides were only about six inches high so he could easily see out, but he still felt cozy and secure. It was very nice having a defined space all his own for a little while. He watched and waited and listened for those tell-tale sounds but heard nothing. The cat stretched and yawned and decided to give himself a wash. Twisting his head, he licked the fur on his back. His rough, pink tongue made long strokes cleaning, smoothing and untangling. He moved on to the long, sleek tail and then his soft, round belly. There was an occasional blast from the guns on deck. Oscar knew from the deep thunderous roar that the main guns were being tested. These four guns had names. Anton and Bruno were the forward guns while Caesar and Dora were in the rear. One by one they fired with long intervals between and then they were silent. Oscar moved on to his head. He licked a paw numerous times and then curled it over his face, flattening his ear, moving down his nose and over his whiskers. This process was repeated several times before the cat switched to the other paw and began working on the other side of his face.

Suddenly a terrific, ear-splitting barrage of heavy gunfire roared out from the main deck. All four of the main guns were fired simultaneously, a full broadside. The cannonade rumbled through the ship, vibrating and echoing even into the far reaches of the darkest corners of the lowest deck. The huge battleship rolled in the Baltic Sea as a result of the blast and some of the lighting in the hallways was knocked out. Oscar leapt out of the box and onto the floor. He stood there in the middle of the officers' wardroom, stunned, shocked and bewildered.

Now this is just too much!! I am really quite put out. Is it truly necessary to test to the absolute limit? Testing is one thing, blowing up the ship in the middle of the sea, is quite another. Here I am doing my duty, keeping out of everyone's way, and I am suddenly victim of the outward display of the power and aggression of mankind...jolted to the very bone.

That's it! As soon as I get out of here, I'm going below decks. I'll find a quiet corner somewhere to rest and settle my nerves. I doubt that I'll even stop by the kitchens later. I don't think I could eat a thing today!

***

Sometime later the door was opened again by Lieutenant Mullenheim-Rechberg who was returning to the officers' wardroom with several others to discuss reports of the testing exercises. Oscar sat waiting in the middle of the room. "No luck hunting today, Oscar?" He asked. "Ah well, the guns must have kept the critters away. But what did you think…very impressive, aren't they?" Oscar could only swish his tail angrily and quickly exit the room. As he departed, he gave his opinion of the full broadside with a short sharp retort. *Mrrrow!!*

CHAPTER SIX

A SHORT EXCURSION

The battleship *Bismarck* departed the Baltic Sea on December 5, 1940, and arrived back at the Blohm & Voss shipyard on December 9, 1940. The following day Oscar decided to take a long walk to shake out his sea legs. After breakfast he trotted down the gangplank onto the familiar dock. It was cold and breezy, and snowflakes danced on the wind while the cat sat, somewhat sheltered between two barrels, surveying the scene. There were several men working the docks, unloading and stacking crates and boxes from a delivery truck. Cranes were busy lifting and swinging goods onto the ship. Ropes and hoses looped from the dock to Bismarck and lay over its side. Oscar saw figures working on deck and an occasional crewman climbing or descending a ladder on the superstructure. Provisioning, maintaining and fine tuning never seemed to stop aboard the great battleship.

A familiar dockworker strode along the dock consulting a clipboard that he carried in his gloved hands. Even though he was wearing a heavy winter coat and a woolen cap pulled down over his ears, Oscar recognized his friend, Johan. He stepped out from between the barrels and stood directly in his path. Johan noticed him immediately and stopped in his tracks. "Well, well, it's you, Oscar. Where have you been? I haven't seen you in ages." Squatting down he pulled off one of his gloves and stroked the cat vigorously. Oscar arched, twisted and turned under his hand and leaned against him affectionately. Johan's rough hands and firm touch felt warm and invigorating.

"You look good, Oscar," Johan continued. "Healthy and well fed. Someone's been taking good care of you. Good for you Oscar. Good for you." A fellow dockworker called and waved to Johan from further along the dock. Johan straightened up pulling his glove on again. "Gotta go, Oscar, duty calls. Good to see you again, little friend." Oscar watched him hurry on to meet with his coworker. The two men bent their heads over the clipboard, nodded in agreement and entered one of the dockside offices.

The snow began falling a little heavier and steadier and the cat raised his face to the sky blinking when snowflakes settled airily on his face. He had better get going. The route was familiar; Oscar had walked it many times before. He left the dock and crossed a wide road. He knew to wait, watch and listen for traffic before he ventured across. He trotted over a bridge and then along a sidewalk lined with tenements, storefronts and eateries. He walked quite a distance before the buildings began to thin out and small single-family homes with little front gardens began to appear. Oscar turned left at an intersection into a residential neighborhood and continued on for another quarter mile. He stopped at an iron gate set in a low brick wall. The cat crouched low and eased under the gate and into the front garden of a small, brick bungalow with a snow-covered front path and a green front door. He followed the path, sat on the front porch, sheltered from the snow shower and waited. He had walked quite a distance, further than the usual territorial range for a cat, but then again, Oscar was an unusual cat with a courageous and adventurous spirit.

An hour or so later a woman stopped at the gate. She was carrying a large bag in each hand and fumbled for a moment to lift the latch and swing it open. Pushing it closed behind her with a foot, she spotted Oscar waiting on the front step. "Oscar. My goodness, we had given you up for lost." She trudged up the path, head angled slightly away from the direction of the snowfall. Placing the bags down with a relieved grunt, she fumbled in her pocket for a key and unlocked the front door. "Well, come on in then," she said without much enthusiasm. "I'll find something for you to eat."

I stayed for the night by the fire where it was warm and cheery. I ate fairly well although the food did not compare to Chief Cook Otto's. Rolf seemed pleased to see me and sat on the floor for a while petting me while asking me where I had been and what I had been doing. They all thought I was back to stay but I, of course, knew better. This was a farewell visit. I had another home now aboard Bismarck, and I knew I would never be coming back again.

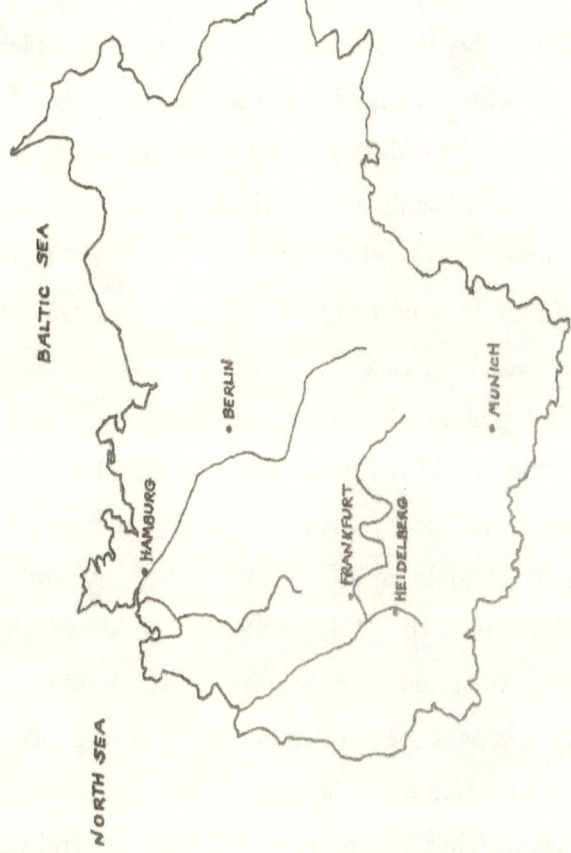

GERMANY AND GERMAN CONTROLLED LANDS — 1941

NORTH SEA

BALTIC SEA

• HAMBURG

• BERLIN

• FRANKFURT

• HEIDELBERG

• MUNICH

CHAPTER SEVEN

CHRISTMAS LEAVE

Later in December the crew was granted Christmas leave. The cat sat watching in the wardroom as many of the sailors packed their duffels while chatting gaily about families, favorite meals and cherished holiday traditions. As the wardroom emptied out, Oscar realized that the ship would not be going anywhere for a while, and he sat dejectedly watching each departure. Steffan approached, cap on head, pea coat buttoned, and duffel slung over his shoulder. "So, my little friend, what do you think? It soon will be Christmas and most of us are going home. I am traveling to Heidelberg to spend the holiday with my parents and little sister, Trina." Oscar rose slowly to his feet and weaved between Steffan's legs bidding him farewell. He sensed the excitement in the young man and was pleased for him even though he would miss him very much during their separation. "It will take several hours to get to Heidelberg, a lot of walking, a bus and a train but it will be wonderful to be back home again for a while." Steffan looked down at the handsome cat and smiled teasingly. "I've written to Trina and told her all about you. She would love to meet you, Oscar…" Steffan grinned. He turned abruptly and picked up a box-shaped object reinforced with leather straps and topped with a sturdy leather handle. "And that is why I am taking you with me, my friend." The young man placed the box in front of Oscar, unhooked a leather latch, and let down a flap which served as a door. It was much like a drawbridge to a castle or the ramp to board a battleship. Inside there was a piece of blanket cut down to size and folded several times to provide comfortable and warm padding. "Karl and I made this carrier for you from some scrap wood and cardboard. What do you think? Come on Oscar…give it a try. If you want to come with me, you'll have to stay inside it for a while." Oscar hesitated before slowly approaching the carrier. He sniffed at it while slowly circling noting the small holes and narrow slits cut into the sides. He stopped at the door flap and looked up at Steffan's smiling expectant face. The cat then stepped cautiously inside, sniffed the blanket and curled up on it. "Hah!" Steffan exclaimed as he closed the flap and fastened the latch and straps. "I knew you would understand, Puss. See fellas?" He said to the small group of seamen who had been watching with interest. "He's a smart cat, is Oscar. Well, everyone, we'll see you in a couple of weeks. Frohe Weihnachten everyone," he called as he picked up the carrier and headed for the exit. "Merry Christmas!"

Steffan invited me to go with him on Christmas leave. What an adventure. The journey was long, but interesting. At first the streets were familiar as Steffan made his way to the bus but after that everything was new. I had never been on a bus before and the ride was rather bumpy and noisy, even though Steffan held the carrier up on his lap and tried his best to cushion the jolts. He talked to me often to calm and reassure me. After a while we left the bus and entered the train station. It was noisy there too. There was quite a crowd on the platform, talking, laughing and calling out to each other. A voice came over the loudspeaker every few minutes and then, when the train came into the station, I was quite amazed at the roar of it and its size as it screeched to a halt. I was not alarmed, though. Having endured the guns aboard Bismarck, the noise of a train paled in comparison. Doors opened and slammed, whistles blew, and we were on our way again. The ride on the train was smoother and faster but a lot longer. We stopped at many train stations along the way where people got off and people got on. A couple of times children peered in at me and asked Steffan my name. "He is Oscar," Steffan answered, "Oscar of the Bismarck."

***

Steffan had his nosed pressed against the window as the train pulled into Heidelberg station. He saw his father and Trina waiting on the platform scanning each window that passed them by as the train slowed to a halt. He waved, jumped from his seat, threw his duffle on his shoulder, grasped the handle of the carrier and made for the door. In seconds he was on the platform, shaking his father's hand and squeezing Trina to his side. "Ah, good to see you, my boy," his father said with a broad smile. "Welcome home…and merry Christmas."

"Steffan, oh Steffan, how handsome you look in your uniform. Mother will be so proud, won't she Papa? She is at home making your favorite dinner. Wait 'til you see the tree, Steffan. It is the biggest we have ever had, and we have decorated it so beautifully, haven't we Papa? We

61

wanted it to be special for you and…oh, look Papa," Trina broke off noticing the box at Steffan's feet. "You *did* bring him, Steffan! It's Oscar!" The girl dropped to her knees on the platform and peered through the slits at the cat.

"Hello, Oscar…hello. I've heard so much about you. You will be spending Christmas with us. I'm *so* glad. Come along, let's get you home." She glanced up at Steffan. "May I carry him, Steffan?"

"Yes, yes you may," Steffan laughed in reply.

The happy little group left the platform and made their way to an older model, but well-kept van. It belonged to Steffan's father who was a fine furniture maker, well-known and respected for his skill in Heidelberg and beyond. The side of the van displayed his name,

Albert Hartmann
Furniture Maker
28 Hillside Avenue
Heidelberg

There was a small, white flower included with the wording, painted beside the "Furniture Maker" line.

It was a short ride home to the house where Steffan had grown up. Almost at the top of a hill, the house was located in a suburb of Heidelberg and commanded a panoramic view of the city. Steffan stood for a moment at the garden gate to take in the familiar scene. The river Neckar gleamed in the winter sunshine as it wove its way northwest to meet the Rhine. The hillsides surrounding the river valley rolled and stretched as far as the eye could see. Thousands of rooftops were clustered together alongside the river in the center of the city but gradually spread further apart as they blended into the suburbs. Far up in the hills the rooftops appeared only occasionally amongst the trees and narrow winding roads. On the south bank of the river Steffan could make out "old town" and its medieval stone bridge and there, above it all, the romantic ruins of Heidelberg Castle. He smiled with pleasure at the stunning view. He was young, home grown and not well traveled but he could not believe that there were many places in the world quite as beautiful as his Heidelberg.

My time at Steffan's home was wonderful. The family made me so welcome. I slept on a warm rug in front of the fire. Trina fussed over me, petted me, and brought her friends in to meet me. There was always something cooking on top of the stove or in the oven. Steffan's mother, Anna, was a very good cook and a variety of tasty meals were mashed or cut up and presented to me in a fine glass dish. (I've never eaten from a glass dish before.) The house was decorated with paper chains and candles and garlands and fruit. In the front parlor, a tall, lush evergreen tree stood sparkling majestically in the sunlight. It was decorated with glittering balls and strewn with silver tinsel. At night it was lit up with colored lights and the family sat in the room in the glow of the tree talking and laughing and singing. I was so happy to be part of it all.

***

As Christmas day approached, brightly wrapped presents accumulated beneath the tree tied with ribbons and bows. Friends and neighbors stopped by to visit bringing cakes and pies, cookies and sweets. Steffan presented Oscar to his friends as his shipmate which earned him much attention and admiration. One day when it snowed, Trina picked the cat up in her arms and took him outside. All was so quiet as the snowflakes drifted down transforming the landscape into a white wonderland. They watched the scene silently for some time until Steffan appeared with two steaming mugs in hand.

"Ah, there you are, you two," he said handing his sister one of the mugs.

"I'm showing Oscar Heidelberg in the snow."

"Ah, yes. What do you think Oscar?" Steffan asked stroking his head. "Beautiful, isn't it? Actually, you know, Heidelberg is beautiful in all seasons. You should see these hillsides in the spring when they are covered with windflowers."

"Oh, Steffan…yes, he *should* see Heidelberg in the spring. Why don't you leave him here with us? I will take good care of him, and he will love the fields and the flowers and the fresh air…and he will chase the butterflies and birds and hunt the field mice. He will be so happy and free…" Steffan smiled fondly at his younger sister and put an arm around her shoulders. "I don't know about that, Trina. Let me think about it…and have a chat with Oscar. We'll see…"

I shall never forget my time here with Steffan's family.

This Christmas is such a happy time. There is so much laughing and singing and eating. There are games and parties, church bells and carols. When the presents are exchanged, everyone is excited, parcels are unwrapped, gifts are admired and there are hugs all around. I received a gift too. Trina placed a box in front of me announcing that it was from all of them, from Albert and Anna and Steffan and Trina. It was my own new blanket, bright blue, fuzzy, soft and warm. Trina placed it in front of the fire, and I curled right up on it, sank into its cozy folds and fell immediately asleep.

***

After Christmas, Albert Hartmann spent some time in his workshop. Years ago, when his business grew too big for his garage, he had designed a workspace, a separate structure off to the side of the house for his woodworking business. He wanted it to be bright and cheery with lots of windows. He hired a contractor and had it built to his speculations. His design rewarded him with a view of the city from the windows in the front of the shop and views of the hillside from the back. When he had moved into the workshop it had been spring and the field behind the shop was covered with windflowers. He decided then that he would incorporate a carved windflower into every one of his pieces to reflect his love of the flower and nature, as well as for appreciation of his good fortune. He now had a thriving business with several employees to help keep up with the demand. Albert Hartmann's reputation had spread, and orders came from all over the country. Recently he had even received a request for a desk from a customer in Switzerland. Purchasers of Albert's work proudly displayed their pieces and took great pleasure in pointing out the windflower so cleverly incorporated into the design.

Oscar found the workshop intriguing. Albert welcomed him in and chatted as he worked. "What do you think, Oscar…a small drawer here for clips and stamps? How about some inlay work on the sides, perhaps a sunburst with a windflower at the center?" He asked with a wink in the cat's direction. Oscar liked the smell of the freshly sawn wood, the curls of wood on the floor, the tiny particles dancing in sunbeams and even the light coating of sawdust beneath his feet. He inspected the pieces all around the shop in various stages of construction before jumping up onto a workbench to watch Albert work and to keep him company.

"I am hoping that Steffan will join me in the business after the war," he told the cat. "I have taught him a lot and he is skilled enough but right now all he talks about is his service, his duty…and the *Bismarck*. I understand that well enough, believe me. Didn't I fight in the last war…?" Albert trailed off pausing in his work for a moment remembering. He took a deep breath and continued on with his task.

"Anyway, I'm hoping Steffan decides to work with me. Love to see him take over the business one day."

So quickly Christmas leave came to an end. The family gathered in the parlor for their farewells. Anna Hartmann gave her son some packages tied with paper and string. "Some things I have knitted for you," she said with a smile. "And some food for you and Oscar for the journey."

"Mama, thank you," Steffan replied planting a kiss on her cheek. "But first we must see what Oscar has decided." He retrieved the cat carrier from the hall closet and placed it on the floor. "Now Oscar," he said. "The choice is yours. You may stay here with the family, or you may come back with me to the *Bismarck*."

All eyes were on the cat as he sat on his blue blanket before the fire. Oscar looked at the family, Anna's gentle, smiling face, Albert's kind, steady gaze and Trina's eager, hopeful expression. Then he looked at Steffan who was dressed in his navy uniform again with his duffle packed and waiting on the floor by his feet.

I understand. Steffan is ready to go back to his duty aboard ship and I am being given the choice to go with him or to remain here with his family. Here, in this delightful, cozy, comfortable, home where I am adored and pampered and well-fed, where I can lay in the sunshine in the warm weather or hunt and explore the nearby hills and dales. Here, where it will be safe and calm and quiet. There is really no choice to make at all!

***

Trina gasped as Oscar slowly rose from his blanket and strode over to the carrier. He looked up once more at all the faces and then stepped inside, curled up and waited.

"Well son," Albert said with a wry smile. "Looks like you have your answer." Steffan bent down to fasten the door, but Trina put a hand on his shoulder. "No, wait

Steffan," she said, her eyes sparkling with unshed tears. "His blanket." She scooped up the blanket, warm from the fire and arranged it inside the carrier around the cat. "Goodbye Oscar," she said simply. "I'll miss you."

Later, on the train, Steffan peered in at his little friend and smiled. "I didn't doubt you for a minute, Oscar," he said. "Not for one minute!"

CHAPTER EIGHT

FINAL SEA TRIALS AND HITLER'S VISIT

The New Year, 1941, arrived on a cold, Siberian wind. The final fitting out of *Bismarck* took place. Eight smaller guns were added, and the battleship was ready to depart again for the Baltic Sea on January 24th. During this time the crew was drilled in combat training. The seamen spent time at battle stations, target shooting, hoisting charges, loading shells and powder. They ran through drills for fire and damage control, response to alarms and bells, securing hatches, closing off compartments and learned communication and reporting procedures. The drills were repeated over and over again. Every possible situation was anticipated, prepared for and practiced so often that the procedures became automatic and routine.

The weeks at the shipyard were quite busy for Oscar. Supplies were delivered daily and consequently more mice and rats came on board also. The cat was eager to be at sea where he could keep the rodent population under control more easily. He also found the constant drills and alarms unsettling and annoying. One afternoon he wandered down to the bakery to inspect the morning delivery of flour and oats. The sacks were stacked in tall, narrow, open compartments ready for the next baking cycle which would begin in a few hours and continue through the night. Two crewmen were carrying and counting clean bread pans and trays as Oscar reached the doorway. The cat noticed immediately that a sack of oatmeal near the bottom of one of the stacks had some loose threads and as he stared, he was amazed to see a small, gray creature, his natural enemy, appear from behind the pile. It scampered up onto the sacks heading toward the loose threads to finish its work creating a hole. Oscar bounded into the room and tore across the floor. The rat saw the danger and in a split second it leapt to the floor and darted away from the cat running around the perimeter of the small room. Oscar pursued and for a few dizzying moments the two animals ran in circles. The cat was unaware of anything else; his whole focus was on the rat with the little black ears. This time he would catch it for sure. The bakery was too small and there were no hiding places. The rat was trapped. It ran frantically but the cat's reflexes were sharper and faster. Oscar stretched out a paw when he was within reach and batted the rat off its stride. The rat staggered, tumbled and rolled across the floor while the cat leapt for the kill. The final victory was spoiled however, by the sudden clatter of heavy, metal bread pans dropped by a crewman who had been unbalanced while attempting to avoid the creatures chasing around beneath his feet. "Och, Puss…watch out!" the sailor cried. Oscar twisted around howling in pain and indignation as one of the pans fell on his tail. The little rat took the opportunity to scamper up over the doorway hatch into a large open space where it disappeared amongst the machinery and equipment stored there. When Oscar roused himself from the battering of the bread pans, he followed over the hatchway and scanned the space beyond, head swiveling back and forth as he searched. There was no sign of the little creature. It had eluded him once again!

My poor tail throbs. I cannot believe my bad luck. I had it! Another second and it would have been all over for that rat. I must catch it. I must. It is my own sworn objective to catch and eliminate that creature. I hate that rat…and my poor tail hurts.

***

On March 6, 1941, *Bismarck* departed again from Hamburg headed for the Baltic Sea. Since the war with Britain had intensified and air raids were more prevalent, three ships accompanied the great battleship as protection against torpedo aircraft and two Me-109 fighters provided air cover the next day during the passage through the Kiel Canal. *Bismarck* ran aground for a while in the canal and had to spend a week docked in Kiel for some work to be done on the underwater hull as well as some bottom painting. On March 14th, the ship was towed to Scheefhagen where provisions were loaded, batteries recalibrated, and two Arado Ar 196 aircraft were brought aboard. Finally, on March 17th, *Bismarck* departed for Gotenhafen for yet more sea trials before its grand mission was to begin.

May 5, 1941 was cool and dry. *Bismarck* was docked at Gotenhafen, and Oscar knew that something special was happening that day. For several days now there had been a lot of extra attention paid to details aboard ship: cleaning and swabbing and shining and polishing of fixtures, windows, decks and equipment. Oscar had heard words spoken repeatedly, "Fuhrer" and "Hitler" in tones of awe, reverence and pride as well as a little anxiety and even fear. By mid-morning the crew was in dress uniform and assembled on deck. Oscar was there too, perched up on the superstructure watching an armored motor yacht approach the ship. As important visitors were piped aboard a standard was raised on the flagstaff, the standard of the Fuhrer, Adolf Hitler. This group of distinguished guests reviewed the crew. The Fuhrer looked rather pale and did not look particularly excited or comfortable aboard. Kommandant Lindemann followed Hitler looking confident and proud and another high-ranking officer accompanied the group, Admiral Lutjens.

Admiral Gunther Lutjens had served Germany's navy for almost thirty years distinguishing himself and rising up the ranks. He was a commander of torpedo boats during World War I and served as Vice Admiral during the invasion of Norway and Denmark in 1940. Late in 1940 he had commanded a raid in the Atlantic and sunk or captured 22 allied vessels. He was recently named the commander of Operation Rheinubung which intended to take all four modern German battleships and battle cruisers, *Bismarck, Scharnhorst, Gneisenau*, and *Tirpitz* on a raid in the Atlantic to sink allied cargo ships. Admiral Lutjens would command the fleet aboard *Bismarck*.

Everyone was assembled on deck to welcome aboard a small group of visitors. The group included Hitler, this Fuhrer that I had been hearing about. He did not look at all as I had imagined. I thought he would be tall, strong, resplendent and I expected him to be excited, animated and charming. He was none of these. I saw a pale, rather short man in a long trench coat who appeared to be only mildly interested in the battleship. He was not at ease aboard ship. This man, I knew, was not a sailing man. I disliked his unattractive mustache, short, narrow, precise and sensed that the Fuhrer was a severe, unkind man. I followed along, out of the way and out of sight, curious to observe him some more.

*** *

The group toured the battleship guided by Lindemann who showed them impressive equipment, control rooms and naval weapon technology. Hitler listened politely as officers in various areas of the ship briefed him on equipment and capabilities, but he had little to say, and his expression was mostly bland. They then spent some time in the admiral's cabin where Admiral Lutjens discussed his experiences in recent action in the Atlantic. He assured Hitler that *Bismarck*'s power and firing precision exceeded that of any British ship. Luncheon followed in the officers' wardroom, a vegetarian one-course meal which was Hitler's preference. After lunch, the Fuhrer spoke about the war. He did not believe that the United States would enter the war, based on the loss of so many American soldiers during World War I and also the unpaid debts of their former allies. Lindemann, however, did not agree with the Fuhrer's viewpoint on the subject of the United States. Admiral Lutjens ended the lunch by talking of the war at sea and of *Bismarck* in particular. He stated that the objective always would be to beat the British wherever they appeared in the oceans.

Hitler and his group departed the battleship four hours after arriving. The visit had been uneventful, stiff and uncomfortable for all.

Up on deck I watched Adolph Hitler disembark as his standard descended the flagstaff. I was happy to see him go. He did not belong aboard our ship. The time he was aboard was not pleasant. Everyone was on edge and routines had been completely disrupted. There is something dark and sinister about that man. He is too powerful. I could tell that he was not enjoying the visit and I hope he never steps foot aboard Bismarck again.

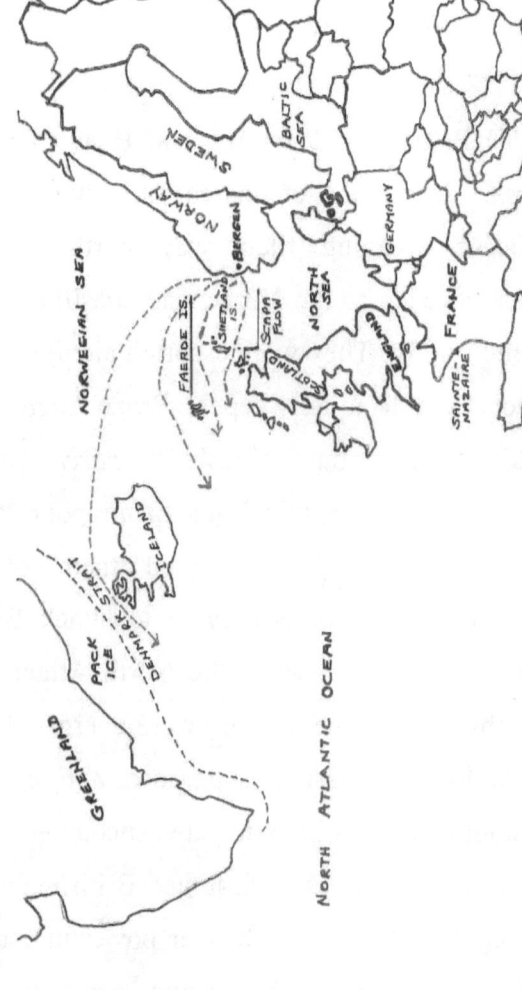

POSSIBLE ROUTES FOR BISMARCK TO THE ATLANTIC

CHAPTER NINE

BISMARCK'S MISSION

On May 19th Battleship, *Bismarck* and Heavy Cruiser, *Prinz Eugen*, departed Gotenhafen en route to the Atlantic Ocean weaving their way north between Denmark and Sweden to the Norwegian coastline where they anchored briefly. They were escorted along the way by destroyers and a minesweeper. *Prinz Eugen* was refueled while at anchor but curiously, *Bismarck* was not. At noon on May 19th, Captain Lindemann spoke to the crew via loudspeaker. He informed them of the destination and mission of *Bismarck*; to attack British shipping and supply convoys in the North Atlantic for several months. The young seamen were energized with the news. At last…a mission, a purpose, ***action***. They speculated confidently about anticipated encounters when they reached the Atlantic. American and British convoys would be easy targets even with their powerful escorts. There was no war ship that could compare with *Bismarck*. Even the "mighty *Hood*" pride of the British fleet, could not match the fire power and strength of the battleship. Karl was a self-taught expert on British ships. He could rattle of dimensions, tonnage, firepower and statistics about a lot of them but especially about *HMS Hood*.

"Built in 1918 and named after Admiral Samuel Hood who served in the American and French Revolutions. He was also a mentor of Nelson," he informed. "42,100 tons, 860 feet long. Can sail 31 knots. Armament includes four twin 15inch guns, thirty-eight anti-aircraft guns, twenty machine guns, five rocket firing mounts and four torpedo tubes. For two decades the Hood has been the most powerful warship ever built. She has sailed all around the world to display her strength and dominance. But, my friends, now she is getting old. She has been refitted several times, but her hull has not been strengthened. She is vulnerable against our guns. She is no longer the queen of the seas."

"*Bismarck* is new and strong. She has state of the art technology, heavier armor and more powerful guns. We have nothing to fear even if we should encounter *Hood*," Steffan stated decisively.

"Oh, it would be a battle indeed," Karl responded. "But you are right, Steffan. We have nothing to fear."

Late in the evening of May 21st, *Bismarck* and *Prinz Eugen* departed Norway and sailed north toward the Denmark Strait, which is the frigid stretch of ocean between Iceland and Greenland. This was the route selected to hopefully evade the British on their way to the Atlantic Ocean. The German battle group was detected, however, several times along their route. Danish and Swedish fishing boats and the Swedish cruiser, *Gotland* sighted the German ships on the 20th of May. *Gotland* reported the sighting, and the information was transmitted to the Admiralty in London. The German ships were also sighted later in the day from the Norwegian coast by a member of the Norwegian resistance who secretly radioed the detection to London. On May 21st, the British sent a plane, a Spitfire, to look for the German ships. The Spitfire spotted the ships off the coast of Norway and photographed them. Britain was very much aware that a battle group including *Prinz Eugen* and, more significantly, *Bismarck,* was on the move and heading for the Atlantic.

Oscar realized that something new was happening. There had been that announcement on the loudspeaker. Everyone had listened intently and chatted excitedly afterwards. Then the crew had gone about their work with renewed energy and a defined purpose and mission. As he had snuggled up to Stefan in his hammock that night, the young seaman had petted him absentmindedly while gazing up at the pipes and ducts overhead. "We are on our way now, Oscar," he said softly. "Looks like we'll see some action soon." The cat purred softly sensing the disquiet and anticipation in his friend and seeking to soothe and comfort with the steady, rhythmic sound.

The ship's cat made his way up to the main deck from time to time as the ship progressed north. He was curious to see the changes in scenery and the sea en route. The color of the ocean varied from green to gray to shades of ice blue. When the coastline came into view, it was dramatic. Massive cliffs and gorges rose severely above the surface and the sea water heaved and smashed heavily onto fallen cliff-face below. Oscar sometimes climbed the superstructure to get a panoramic view and to see the other ships in the battle group escorting the great *Bismarck* on her way. They were an impressive sight, these powerful warships with their ominous guns pointing the way to anticipated action at sea and their white wakes churning behind them. The clever cat was putting it together. He watched and listened and learned. *Bismarck* and *Prinz Eugen* were going on a hunt. First, they had to get to their hunting ground without being detected and then they would hunt and attack and destroy their prey. There was risk, of course. The prey would counter-attack to defend but the great *Bismarck* was bigger and stronger than its prey and was sure to be victorious.

As this great ship embarks on its mission, I must recommit to my own. I must devise a strategy to find and destroy that rat. For the next few days, I will look for clues to learn its routine, its usual path and its hiding places. Then, I will decide where to lay in wait to catch the creature out in the open when it is unsuspecting and unprotected.

***

The hunt was on. The British knew now that the *Bismarck* was on the move toward the Atlantic Ocean. This great, powerful, threatening battleship had to be stopped. But which way would it go? There were several routes that Admiral Lutjens could choose. He could pass between the Orkney Islands and the Shetland Islands off the coast of Scotland, but he would be too close to the British naval base at Scapa Flow. For the same reason Lutjens rejected passing between the Faeroe Islands and the Shetland Islands. He could navigate two ways around Iceland, to the northwest between Iceland and Greenland through a part of the ocean known as the Denmark Strait; or to the southeast between Iceland and the Faeroe Islands.

The British Admiral, Tovey, ordered the Battle Cruiser, *Hood* and Battleship, *Prince of Wales* into position south of Iceland to cover the Denmark Strait route as well as the Faeroes-Iceland passage. The heavy cruisers, *Norfolk* and *Suffolk*, were directed to the Denmark Strait and three light cruisers were directed to patrol the Faeroes-Iceland passage. Admiral Tovey formed a second task force with ships still at Scapa Flow. This task force consisted of the battleship *King George V*, the aircraft carrier *Victorious*, the battle cruiser *Repulse*, five light cruisers, *Aurora*, *Galatea*, *Hermione*, *Kenya*, and *Neptune* and six destroyers.

Late on May 22nd the fleet departed to wait in the ocean northwest of Scotland, behind the light cruisers, ready to pounce on *Bismarck* if it appeared in the Faeroes-Iceland passage. The fleet could also sail westward from its position to support *Hood* and *Prince of Wales* if *Bismarck* should elect to pass though the Denmark Strait.

I have thought about the places where I have encountered the rat and the times of day that I have seen it. I am putting together a route and a timeline in my mind; one that I think the rat may be following to access food at times when certain locations are not manned. I believe that the creature arrives in Otto's kitchen pantry very late at night when the kitchen is quiet...perhaps only one or two staff laying out utensils and measuring ingredients for the breakfast meal. I will hide and observe for a night or two and plan my surprise attack.

***

Lutjens made the decision to take the Denmark Strait route. *Bismarck* sailed north followed by *Prinz Eugen* and the three destroyers. In the early morning of May 22nd, the destroyers were released and turned to the east heading back to Norway. The two capital ships continued on through difficult weather conditions. The day remained, cloudy, rainy and very foggy. Just after noon, the submarine and air alarm sounded, and the ships zigzagged for a while in response. Soon after that in an effort to be less identifiable to enemy aircraft, the turrets were painted over, and canvas was spread on decks to cover the swastikas.

Oscar sat for a while on the superstructure watching the activity below on deck. Sailors were unrolling and spreading huge canvases on the deck as others climbed atop the turrets carrying cans of paint and brushes. He thought it was not a good day for painting. The weather was miserable. Low, dark clouds covered the sky creating a cold, dull atmosphere and moisture hung in the air as the clouds lowered forming a dense fog. Just as *Bismarck* turned on her searchlight, Oscar decided to go below. There was nothing to see today.

I made my rounds watching for signs of the rat with the little black ears. I saw nibbles here, new holes there and I'm becoming familiar with his routine. I saw him in the kitchen last night. It was all I could do not to lurch from my hiding place and lunge towards him. But I reminded myself, I was conducting an observation exercise and would soon know exactly how and when to strike. I watched the rat appear and scamper over the threshold. It hesitated, sniffed the air and scanned the room before it scurried along the floor keeping tight against the wall heading for the pantry. At the door to the pantry, it stopped again, sniffed and approached the threshold. Its little head darted in all directions before it climbed over and inside. Who is it that leaves the door of the pantry ajar?

***

Two British light cruisers, *Norfolk* and *Suffolk* had been dispatched a few days earlier to monitor the Denmark Strait. They tracked *Bismarck* and *Prinz Eugen* using radar as the German ships entered the Denmark Strait navigating through overcast, rain, fog and intermittent heavy snow showers. Ahead, in the direction of Greenland, the crew could see high glaciers in the background and fields of bluish pack ice stretching for miles and miles. To port, in the direction of Iceland, a heavy haze hung over the water.

Tensions increased aboard *Bismarck* as the day wore

on. The crew knew that the strait alone was dangerous as it narrowed and contained ice bergs, pack ice and fog. But there was also the fear of encountering enemy ships at any time on the way out to the Atlantic. At just after 18:00 alarm bells sounded, and the ships turned to starboard as lookouts reported vessels to port. These turned out to be icebergs created by ice spurs and floes that had piled on top of each other forming ominous shapes. At almost 19:30 alarms sounded again. This time radar had picked up a contact to port. When the silhouette of a cruiser, *Suffolk*, came into view, Lutjens realized that they were being trailed from behind and knew that *Suffolk* had radioed their position back to British naval command. At 20:30 another contact was made. *Norfolk* had sailed closer to the German ships than she had meant to, and *Bismarck's* guns fired. Huge splashes landed in the water around *Norfolk* who laid down smoke and promptly disappeared into the fog. With this sighting and first shots fired, there was now no doubt aboard the German ships that a battle lay ahead.

During the evening two significant events occurred. *Bismarck* changed positions with *Prinz Eugen* because *Bismarck's* forward radar was disabled by the blast while firing at *Norfolk* and around 22:00 Bismarck suddenly reversed in an attempt to catch *Suffolk* unexpectedly. However, *Suffolk* withdrew, and *Bismarck* returned to formation behind *Prinz Eugen*.

It was an unsettling evening. I had made my way to the kitchen where Otto gave me my dinner. He and two men were laying out pots and pans and stacking plates and dishes in readiness for the next day's meal. The three men worked quickly and quietly. When the alarm sounded the men froze in place for a moment. Instructions came over the loudspeaker. I heard "Gefechtsstationen!(battle stations)" Plates and pots were set down with a clatter as the men ran for the door hatch. They were over, through and gone in only seconds. I watched them go and then turned back to finish my dinner quickly. I had a pretty good idea that there would be guns blasting before too long.

I was in the pantry cleaning myself after my meal when the guns fired. I was startled and alert, but I didn't jump out of my skin as I had in the past. Guess I knew I was on a warship and expected to hear guns once in a while. I just hunkered down and waited.

This engagement did not last long. Only five salvos

and it was over. I stayed a while longer in the pantry and then stretched, yawned and headed to the wardroom to wait for Steffan.

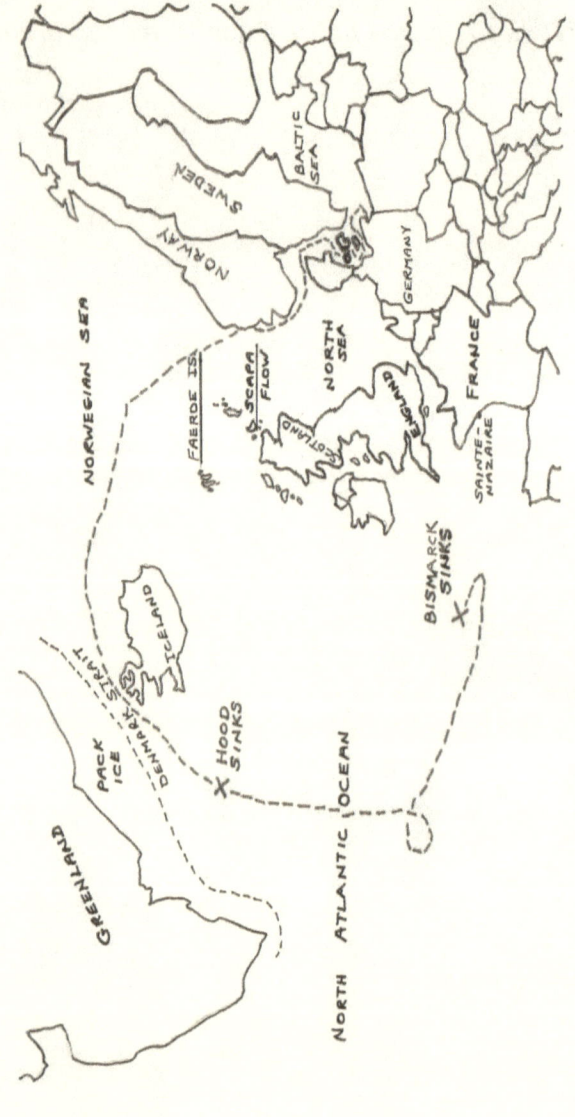

ROUTE OF BISMARCK

CHAPTER TEN

LOSS OF *HMS HOOD* AND THE HUNT FOR *BISMARCK*

The sun rose early, and the weather was clear on the morning of May 24th. Steffan tumbled from his hammock when alarm bells sounded and "**Battle stations**" was ordered through the loudspeakers. All the men in the wardroom raced for the hatchways and headed for their stations. Oscar waited for the wardroom to empty and then he made his way topside. On deck, he gloried for a moment in the brilliant sunrise and clear skies before deftly climbing a few levels of the superstructure and jumping into a lifeboat. From there, he had a commanding view of the situation.

Prinz Eugen was now ahead of *Bismarck* and far off to the port beam, there were two large, enemy ships. Oscar watched the ships slowly grow larger and larger as they approached. The crew was desperately trying to identify the ships when the British guns opened fire. At 5:53 a.m. first shots were fired. The battle cruiser *Hood* fired at *Prinz Eugen* under the direction of Vice-Admiral Holland who thought that it was *Bismarck* since it was the forward ship. Captain Leach aboard the *Prince of Wales* realized that the second ship was *Bismarck* and fired at the second German ship. Great columns of water rose from the surface of the sea as the salvos exploded. The shots all missed their targets. *Prince of Wales* adjusted its range and shot again at *Bismarck*. *Hood* shot again at *Prinz Eugen* still believing it to be *Bismarck*. The shots all missed.

Guns from the enemy ships are firing at us! The shots have all missed but have created immense waterspouts all around us. I am fearful but intrigued and I feel quite safe in the lifeboat. I am also quite secure in the knowledge that Bismarck is the superior battleship. These enemy ships do not realize what they are up against. The magnificent Bismarck will fire back and blow them out of the water.

***

But *Bismarck* did not fire back immediately. Lutjens was still considering his primary orders, to get to the Atlantic to sink supply ships, not to engage British warships.

Vice-Admiral Holland realized his error in believing that the lead ship was *Bismarck* and changed his target from *Prinz Eugen* to *Bismarck*. More salvos fired at *Bismarck* as a shout of recognition spread around the ship. "*Hood*! The *Hood*…it's the *Hood*!"

Gunnery officers were requesting permission to fire, but permission was not granted. Lutjens was hesitating. And then suddenly, Kommandant Lindemann who had been desperately waiting for Lutjens's order, muttered to himself, "I will not let my ship be shot out from under my ass." He came on the intercom and gave the much-awaited order, "Permission to fire!"

A short, tragic and decisive battle at sea ensued. Both German ships fired at *Hood* for about four minutes before Lutjens ordered *Prinz Eugen* to direct fire on *Prince of Wales*. *Hood* had taken a hit from *Prinz Eugen* and was on fire amidships. *Prince of Wales* hit *Bismarck* causing an oil leak. *Bismarck* hit *Hood*. *Prince of Wales* hit *Bismarck* below the waterline where several compartments were flooded and damaged. At this point an RAF plane, *Sunderland*, emerged from the clouds and flew over *Hood*. It reported fires in two places. *Prince of Wales* hit *Bismarck* a third time. At 06:00 *Hood* suddenly exploded as a tall flume of flame shot upward. A magazine, or torpedoes, or propellant must have ignited causing a catastrophic and fatal eruption. The ship broke into two pieces and the end came swiftly. *Hood* fired a last salvo from her forward guns, her stem stood high in the air and then she disappeared below the surface of the sea. *Bismarck* now directed its guns at *Prince of Wales*. The RAF airplane *Sunderland* moved toward the German ships and received anti-aircraft fire from *Bismarck*. *Prince of Wales* fired again at *Bismarck* who returned fire and scored a big hit killing almost everyone on the compass platform. The airplane returned to the clouds to escape the heavy anti-aircraft fire. At just 06:03 *Hood* was sunk, and *Prince of Wales* was developing a smoke screen as it attempted to flee. *Bismarck* and *Prinz Eugen* continued to fire as she fled but also were responding to aircraft and torpedo alarms and so turned away from her. *Prince of Wales* returned fire but was not very accurate because of the loss of the compass platform. The brief battle ended at 06:10. Kommandant Lindemann had wanted to finish off the *Prince of Wales,* but Lutjens refused, committed again to his standing orders not to engage enemy ships except those defending supply convoys. He was also concerned that he could encounter other British warships if he pursued the *Prince of Wales*.

It all happened so fast. Suddenly our guns began firing at the two enemy ships. I heard salvos from Prinz Eugen also. I felt the superstructure tremble and vibrate with the powerful force of the guns and huge fountains of seawater erupted all around us. Several times I felt a different vibration and somewhat muffled explosion below and I knew we had been hit. Then there were cheers. Cheers and whoops spread throughout the ship, and I saw far off in the ocean, smoke and fire spewing from the remains of an enemy ship. The Hood had exploded! I was pleased for the crew and my friends aboard Bismarck for this successful strike and kill. But, as I gazed at the battle cruiser, broken, burning and sinking, I realized that there were men aboard, men much like, Steffan, and Otto, Karl, Conrad, Kommandant Lindemann, and Admiral Lutjens. Many, many, young crewmen were dead and dying on the demolished British ship. Perhaps there had been a cat on board too...like me. I hunkered down in the lifeboat when an airplane buzzed around us for a while like an annoying fly and I listened to the sounds of the battle as it wound down. The gunfire became more and more sporadic and return fire came from farther and farther away. When the firing stopped completely, I peered over the side of the lifeboat. The shape of an enemy ship moving away appeared from time to time through a smoky fog. But we did not purse. The battle was over.

***

When Oscar returned below deck later in the morning, he passed the officers' wardroom and witnessed a brief victory celebration. The gunnery officers, including Mullenheim-Rechberg, were congratulated on their skill and the successful shots which resulted in the sinking of the mighty British battle cruiser, *Hood*. The officers celebrated with a glass of champagne. In the lower wardroom off-duty crewmen talked excitedly. The famous *Hood* had been sunk so swiftly and decisively. What a victory for *Bismarck* and her crew. Oscar walked the perimeter of the room looking for Steffan but finding that he was not there, he hunched down in a corner to wait for him. The young crewmen relived the short battle from their various viewpoints and battle stations. The whoops and animated gestures subsided after a while as the talk turned to the hits that *Bismarck* had received and the extent of the damage to the ship. Would it be enough to change or delay the mission? The men did not think so.

Mid-morning, Steffan returned to the wardroom. He stripped off his damp overalls which were filthy with grease and grime and slumped in a chair. Oscar rose, stretched and strolled over to his friend leaping gracefully into his lap. Steffan absentmindedly stroked the cat from his head to his tail and then scratched him under his chin. He had been part of a damage control work party and the compartments he inspected had serious problems. Oil was leaking, pumps were under water and valves in the oil lines were not working. Some temporary measure had been taken to close up holes in the hull but he was quite sure that permanent repairs would have to be made. The crew in the wardroom gathered round Steffan anxious to hear his assessment of the situation.

"Don't see how we can continue on, fellas." He stated. "She needs quite a bit of patching up." And indeed, around noon *Bismarck* changed course and word spread around the ship that the operation in the Atlantic would have to be postponed.

Admiral Lutjens decided to release *Prinz Eugen* and allow her to continue on to the Atlantic on her own. Later in the day, to ensure that the ship got away undetected, Lutjens ordered *Bismarck* to turn and sail directly at *Norfolk* and *Suffolk* who were still tracking the German ships. At a distance of ten miles, *Bismarck* emerged from the fog guns blazing. The British cruisers had to break away and *Prinz Eugen* was able to escape out of range of British radar. Now, *Bismarck* was alone at sea, damaged, leaking, and vulnerable as she headed west toward a French port for repairs.

The following day, Lutjens addressed the men of *Bismarck*.

Seamen of the battleship Bismarck! You have covered yourself with glory! The sinking of the battle cruiser Hood has not only military, but psychological value, for she was the pride of England. Henceforth the enemy will try to concentrate his forces and bring them into action against us. I, therefore, released Prinz Eugen at noon yesterday so that she could conduct commerce warfare on her own. She has managed to evade the enemy. We, on the other hand, because of the hits we have received, have been ordered to proceed to a French port. On our way there the enemy will gather and give us battle. The German people are with you, and we will fight until our gun barrels glow red-hot and the last shell has left the barrels. For us, seamen, the question is victory or death.

***

Morale was high on May 25th in spite of an attack the night before of eight Swordfish torpedo bombers from the British carrier *Victorious*. Only one of the torpedoes launched at *Bismarck* resulted in a hit and caused no serious damage. Not long after this air attack *Bismarck* eluded her pursuers. The British ships were zigzagging as they shadowed the German battleship to evade German U-boats that they feared were in the area and during one zig, *Bismarck* conducted a maneuver which resulted in a successful escape from her pursuers. The British ships had lost *Bismarck*!

***

For thirty hours *Bismarck* was undetected by the British. Although Admiral Lutjens made a grievous error and sent two long radio transmissions to German headquarters which were intercepted by the British, the staff aboard battleship *King George V* also made an error calculating *Bismarck*'s position. The British believed that *Bismarck* was headed north to the narrow between Iceland and the Faroe Islands and all ships were ordered to an intercept course north. Meanwhile, *Bismarck* sailed south and gained a distance of one hundred and fifty miles from the British ships.

It is quiet again. I am back to my old routine. The crew is still watchful and edgy but as each hour passes and there is no sign of the enemy, tensions are beginning to ease. Chief cook Otto greeted me earlier when I appeared in the galley in his old, affectionate manner. "Ah…Matrose Oscar, my little miezekatze, here you are. Come for your dinner. Well, let me see what I have for you." Otto busied himself selecting morsels from various cauldrons talking all the while. "We got the Hood, Oscar. It took no time at all. She went up like a firecracker. What a strike! What a victory…eh, Oscar? And now we sail away. Got to get a few repairs and then we'll be at it again. What a ship, Oscar! What a ship, Bismarck, eh, Oscar?" He placed a dish on the floor and stroked me as I ate. "Of course, we can't sail at full speed because of the damage, and we are leaving a bit of an oil slick behind us…" Otto trailed off. I stopped eating for a moment to nuzzle his hand. I could tell he was worried in spite of his bravado. "Ah, good Puss…good Puss," he said.

I had a pleasant day on my rounds checking all the food storage areas. I spent a little time with Conrad below in the storage room as he straightened and organized supplies that had shifted during the battle. I watched carefully in case a mouse or perhaps even the rat scurried out from behind a sack. "Thanks, Oscar," Conrad said as he gathered some supplies to bring up to the kitchen. "Always good to have your company." I like Able Seaman Conrad.

The men were in good cheer below in the wardroom. I arrived there in the early evening as they were slinging hammocks. A lot of the men greeted me, and some stopped to give me a quick pat or stroke. Steffan scooped me up and set me on his hammock where I stretched and rolled and then curled up to sleep. I listened for a while to the sounds of the wardroom, scraping of chairs, flop of pillows and blankets chatter and banter of the men, *shuffling of cards, and then the sounds blended into a jumble of soothing background noise lulling me into a deep sleep.*

***

Although the day was dull and cloud cover was low in the sky on the morning of May 26th, the crew was optimistic that they had eluded the enemy. Word got around that the British force was more than 100 miles away and that by the next day *Bismarck* would be close enough to the French coast to be in range of the Luftwaffe's (German air force) protection. The battleship was moving at reasonable speed and had a good chance of reaching St. Nazaire, a French port, before being detected.

At 10:30 however, the hopes of the crew were dashed. A British airplane, a PBY Catalina, which had left its base in North Ireland on a scouting mission, suddenly appeared below the clouds. The flying boat with the long, straight wing and propellers above the cabin had been following the oil trail left by *Bismarck*. The pilot of the Catalina radioed the position of the German warship back to base as *Bismarck* opened fire on the airplane. The

Catalina disappeared again into the clouds leaving the crew disheartened and dismayed by their discovery.

At the time of the sighting of *Bismarck* by the Catalina, the British battleship, *Rodney* was 125 miles southeast and *King George V* was 135 miles south of the German battleship. Force H, consisting of the aircraft carrier, *Ark Royal*, battle cruiser *Renown*, and cruiser *Sheffield* were heading north from Gibraltar and an escort of destroyers were recalled from convoy duty and ordered to meet up with *Rodney* and *King George V*. The destroyers consisted of *Cossack, Maori, Zulu, Sikh, and Piorun*. Along with heavy cruiser, *Dorsetshire, Prince of Wales* (damaged but still involved), *Norfolk* and *Suffolk* and aircraft carrier *Victorious*, this mighty and determined British force consisting of 2 aircraft carriers, 3 battleships, 1 battle cruiser, 3 heavy cruisers, and 5 destroyers, all now pursuing *Bismarck*, pride of the German navy and sinker of *Hood*.

Oscar was up on deck for his evening stroll when fifteen Swordfish torpedo planes from the *Victorious* dove out of low clouds and flew over the ship. The alarm sounded, loud and insistent, as Oscar hurried to the confines of the same lifeboat where he had endured the confrontation with *Hood*. Anti-aircraft guns sounded immediately as well as some of the turret guns, but the aircraft flew in low around the ship and were not easy targets for *Bismarck*'s mounted guns. Oscar peered out from the lifeboat, eyes large and wide as the sights, sounds and smells of the battle assaulted his senses. The antique-looking biplanes rushed past the ship droning and buzzing like angry bees. Each carried a single torpedo which hung below the cabin of the plane, large, imposing, an ominous threat to *Bismarck* and all those aboard. Guns continued firing furiously at the planes. Smoke filled the air. Splashes of torpedoes hitting the water were followed by rapid maneuvers as Captain Lindemann bellowed commands on the bridge attempting to dodge the approaching "eels". "All ahead full!" "All stop!" "All full back!" "Ahead!" "All stop!" Several streaks of white bubbling water hissed past missing their target as the ship heeled, slowed and lurched to evade impact. A sudden explosion forward on the bow sent a shuddering vibration through the ship. Oscar recoiled and hunkered down on the floor of the lifeboat for the duration. Two planes came in very low and headed toward the stern while others on the port side turned right toward the stern also.

The last of the torpedoes were loosed and resulted in a hit on stern. The explosion that followed caused critical damage which would soon become apparent to the captain and crew and the Swordfish, their job done, flew away.

The crew, at first, breathed a sigh of relief although they remained at their stations in case of another attack. The damage did not appear to be too severe and damage-control parties went to work immediately. Some compartments were flooded, and water was pumped out, rooms were sealed off, leaks were repaired. However, the torpedo attack in the stern had hit the rudder, jamming it in a fixed position and causing the ship to circle. Attempts were made to repair it, remove it, disengage it, but all failed. Even the valiant effort of divers, who desperately worked at the rudder coupling, was unsuccessful. They could not budge it. Captain Lindemann tried using the propellers and speed adjustments to steer and was able to manage a little maneuvering that way, but the increasing wind and rising seas counteracted his efforts. *Bismarck* was, in fact, drifting slowly northwesterly back the way they had come and towards the British fleet. To top it off, a storm developed throughout the evening blowing to the northwest.

It was a bad night. The crew was on edge at their stations as the realization of the peril of their situation began to sink in. They knew that heroic attempts at repairs and alternate, compensating procedures were on-going and hope bubbled up from time to time when something new was enacted. Although the crew was not informed of the details and extent of the damage, the obvious maneuverings and limitations of the ship told the tale. At 23:00 British destroyers were spotted, and alarm bells sounded yet again. *Bismarck*'s guns fired toward the enemy, but they were hard to see due to the blackness of the night and the driving rain. Neither the number of destroyers nor their identities could be determined. At 01:00 on May 27th a star shell was launched from a destroyer briefly lighting up the scene on the ocean. These star shells were used periodically throughout the night and shots from the destroyers' guns continued at intervals during the dark hours. The British were obviously keeping *Bismarck* in view, and the crew disheartened until daybreak.

I waited for a while at the bottom of the lifeboat after the guns had stopped shooting and the engines of the airplanes had faded away. It was eerily quiet following the attack. I heard only the sound of the sea and the rush of the wind. I could see men still at their posts when I peered out of the boat, waiting and watching, tense and twitchy. When some time passed with no more action I jumped over the side of the boat and made my way down to the deck. I slunk, low to the ground peering up fearfully at the darkening sky once or twice as I made my way along. Below deck, I soon realized that I could not conduct my rounds as usual. Some areas were completely abandoned, the wardrooms, the kitchen, the storerooms, but a few crewmen occupied the radio room, focused intently, leaning forward on the edge of their seats at their desks, and damage control parties were hurrying about carrying clipboards, papers and folders. I encountered sea water in one compartment and heard the pumps at work while men shouted information and instructions back and forth. I did manage to get down to the engine room and found Steffan, hot and grubby, busily working on valves and checking gauges. All the men in the engine room were focused on their jobs, scurrying around, checking pressures, tightening, adjusting, cleaning, periodically wiping the sweat from their faces and calling out readings. I watched for a while aware of the tension and apprehension as the men worked dutifully at their activities and I realized for the first time that all was not well on the Bismarck.

***

Steffan and the engine room crew worked frantically throughout the night to keep the engines in top working order since Captain Lindemann was putting extra strain on them using the propellers to steer the ship as best he could. The crew knew that the rudder was not operational and that various efforts were continuing to repair the damage. Steffan was hopeful that the efforts would succeed but he was also very concerned for his fate and that of the *Bismarck* and all the crew. He would do his duty and work as hard as he could at his own post to assist in the effort. While moving along the length of the compartment checking pressure readings, he spotted Oscar watching from a dark corner. He paused, smiled and approached the cat who came forward to greet his friend. Steffan squatted and scratched his visitor around the ears and neck.

"Ah, Oscar. So…you have come to see me, have you? It is good to see you… always good to see you puss. How are you doing through all this, eh, Oscar?" Oscar nuzzled and purred and rubbed up against him. He wanted to comfort the young man. He could sense the heightened state of nerves and anticipation in the crewman. Steffan stroked the cat along the length of his back all the way to the end of his tail several times before he spoke again.

"Now Oscar, as you can see, we are busy down here. Not a good place for you to stay. Go on now. Up to the wardroom with you. I'll see you there later." Steffan rose and stood up looking down at him. "Off you go now," he said gently. Oscar hesitated for a moment not wanting to leave. He wanted to curl up in a corner out of the way content to watch the activity or take a nap in spite of the thrum of the engines and hissing of pipes. But his friend had told him to leave and so leave he must. He headed to the hatch looking back when he reached it. Steffan was already striding away, pulling a rag from the back pocket of his trousers and wiping his hands as he called a question to one of the crew. Oscar stepped through the hatch and wondered if he would ever see his friend again.

The cat made his way back to the kitchen. He decided to wait there in case anyone came down. Perhaps he would get a tidbit or two. Oscar waited there a long time. He lay down, curled up and dozed on and off for several hours waking as information and updates were relayed to the crew over the loudspeaker.

The crew was told of the efforts to repair the rudder, of on-going repairs to leaks and damage on the ship, of U-boats that were heading toward *Bismarck* to provide protection, and of messages from the Luftwaffe that bombers were on their way. Morale amongst the men lifted with these reports. The men were hopeful that the rudder would be repaired and that with the help of U-boats and bombers, *Bismarck* would be able to make its way back to France. They cheered each other up, chatted optimistically and waited. However, when an announcement was made just after midnight that the rudder was irreparably jammed and that all work on it had stopped, spirits fell low and the men began to realize that the ship and their own lives were doomed.

01:53 Message read to the crew of *Bismarck* from Adolf Hitler: "All Germany is with you. What can be done, will be done. Your performance of duty will strengthen our people in the struggle for its destiny."

***

Later in the night the crew heard an announcement that permitted everyone to help himself to anything that he wanted from the kitchen, storerooms and the ship's store. It was received with dismay as it could only mean that Lutjens, Lindemann and the ship's officers knew that the end was near. However, intermittent reports of U-boats, planes, a tanker and ocean tugs on the way built up hopes again. The loudspeaker sounded repeatedly, "Watch for our planes." "Watch for our U-boats."

Chief cook Otto hurried to his kitchen to spread out food for the men. Bread, rolls and pastries were brought from the bakery, meat, cheese, fruit and beer were taken out of cold storage. Eggs and bacon were soon cooking on the stovetops. Coffee was brewing. He worked fast directing his kitchen crew as they joined him from their battle stations, remembering special supplies, chocolate, ice cream, cake, champagne and he laid it all out. Plates, forks, mugs were brought out and the crew began to trickle down to the kitchen for a quick bite and a mug of brew. Otto watched them come in, some dazed, some dejected, some putting on a brave face, some trying to make jokes, some clinging to hope. He made sure everything was available.

"Dig in boys," he cried. "There's plenty more so eat all you want. What a feast…eh, boys? What a feast!" He worked for hours replenishing, cooking, brewing, pouring, and at times leaning back against a counter with a satisfied but melancholy smile as he watched the best of his stores being scooped up, drunk and devoured. He would do his duty to the last. No sailor aboard *Bismarck* would be hungry or wanting while he had charge of the kitchens…especially now, he thought…especially now.

During one of his brief pauses, Otto noticed Oscar sitting in a corner of the compartment watching the activity. He broke into a broad smile picked up a small dish and began filling it with tasty morsels.

"Nein, nein, Otto does not forget his little miezekatze," he called to him. "Matrose Oscar shall have his special feast too. Look what I have for you, some tasty sausage and chicken…a little fish too. Ach, how about a shrimp on top? That's nice, isn't it Puss?" The cook added a spoonful of jellied fish stock from cold storage and presented his creation to the cat who had been focused on Otto, watching with close interest. Oscar meowed a quick, thank you, rubbed briefly against his friend's legs and tucked in.

Ah, what a special treat. The assortment of flavors is astonishing, wonderful, glorious. I eat here on the floor of the kitchen while men file past carrying their plates to the wardroom, the kitchen crew dart about with pitchers of beer, and Otto produces more cauldrons, pots and platters. From time to time, I hear distant guns and explosions and notice the men abruptly freeze as they listen intently to the ominous sounds with dread and foreboding. None of the shells seem to reach us, however. We do not suffer any hits.

As the early hours of the morning progress, the men drift away, back to their posts. They are tired, not having slept in several days, but they are anxious and eager to do their duty to man their stations, to shoot, fight, prevail. I watch them all leave until the kitchen and wardroom are empty again. Otto is the last one to leave. He stands for a moment, hands on hips looking about the kitchen, at the clutter and the remnants of food and platters to be scraped, washed and put away. He sighs deeply, wipes his hands on a cloth by the sink and deserts his kitchen to return above deck. I feel sorry for my friend as I watch him go. I am worried about him, worried about all the men, and about myself. What is to become of us all? Daylight is just a few hours away. I don't think it is going to be a very good day.

Sometime later after nibbling some more of my sumptuous supper, while washing my whiskers, I catch a sudden movement out of the corner of my eye. I freeze as my predatory instincts respond immediately and I feel the fur rise up from my back. It is the rat! Sniffing, then stopping, then scurrying across the floor, it makes its way to the long counter where food left abandoned and untended are easy pickings. I watch as it scampers up the side of the lower cupboards onto the countertop and towards the remains of a side of ham. The animal tears a piece away with its teeth, then holds it between its front feet and nibbles at it hungrily. I am outraged! Forgotten is the danger we face, the fate of the ship, the peril of the crew. I am oblivious to the booming of shells, explosions, and geysers of seawater in the ocean around us. I am aware solely of the rat scavenging so brazenly, now back on its haunches reaching for another piece, its tiny, black ears perky and clearly visible on its bold little head.

CHAPTER ELEVEN

ALL IS LOST

Dawn broke on May 27th, 1941, to gray skies, churning seas, heavy rain and howling wind. The great German battleship, *Bismarck,* drifted northwest hurried along by impatient gusts. The crew waited, miserable but brave, apprehensive but hopeful, weary but alert at their stations, manning guns, turrets, range finders, engine rooms, turbine rooms, powder rooms, and ammunition rooms. Men above decks turned their eyes repeatedly to the sky seeking the promised air support from the Luftwaffe. They had heard a report that fifty-one bombers had taken off at 05:20. They scanned the swelling waves and restless sea for periscopes. Where were the U-boats that had been speeding to their location? Admiral Lutjens and Captain Lindemann and ship's officers were on the bridge gazing through their binoculars and sweeping the horizon, scouring the skies for the expected bombers as they prepared to command *Bismarck* during the impending battle at sea.

A few minutes after 08:30 smoke clouds were detected

through the rain and gloom and alarm bells sounded. As the ships approached, the silhouettes could be identified as British battleships, *King George V* and *Rodney*. *Rodney* peeled off to port heading easterly to engage *Bismarck* from a different angle and was the first to fire. *King George V* fired a minute later. *Bismarck* returned fire against *Rodney*. The heavy cruiser, *Norfolk* fired against *Bismarck*. None of these shots were successful. It seemed that the British ships were having trouble finding the correct range. However, at 09:02 *Bismarck* was hit for the first time. It was a spectacular hit by *Rodney* on the forward section of the German battleship which resulted in a huge jolt along the ship, the spewing of wood and steel and raging fires as stores of ammunition blew up below decks. A couple of minutes later, heavy cruiser *Dorsetshire* began firing at *Bismarck*. The British were firing from all directions causing horrific damage and destruction.

The final battle was on, and *Bismarck* was at a distinct disadvantage. It could not maneuver and had no support. Although U-boats and bombers had been promised, none appeared (one U-boat did eventually arrive in the area but it had no torpedoes and so could not help.) The men aboard the mightiest battleship ever afloat were desperately working to keep *Bismarck* in the fight. They stayed at their stations performing their duties until it became impossible as the ship took hit after hit. Brave men rushed to help wherever they could when their own stations were damaged and could no longer function. Young crewmen died horribly in massive explosions. Bodies and body parts were strewn about the deck and superstructure. Giant holes appeared all over the ship, smoke and flames rose up from below decks in raging infernos. Men screamed and shouted trying to help fallen comrades, lifting debris, staunching wounds, slinging arms of bleeding, broken men over their shoulders and seeking areas of shelter. And still *Bismarck*'s guns were firing. Still orders were coming down from the bridge.

"Shoot!"

"Fire!"

"Port engines half ahead, starboard engines back slow!"

"A damage control party to battery deck, compartment ten!"

"Damage report – team 4. How close is the fire to the ammo storage?"

"Close bulkhead doors to the central turbine room!"

Some of these orders and questions were heard and answered, others were not.

Bismarck was a floating, smoking, mangled wreck but her turrets still continued to fire until one by one they took hits resulting in huge, rocking jolts throughout the ship. The guns were blown completely off or were frozen at useless angles, pointing aimlessly at the sky or hanging awkwardly on the deck. At 09:40 *Bismarck* lost its last turret and the great battleship fell silent.

Now a dreaded order was received by the crew; the order was given to scuttle the ship. Crewmen who had fought so bravely to save the ship now found themselves forced to sink it. Bulkhead doors and hatches were ordered to be opened and demolitions charges were set. Demolition parties clambered through debris and smoke to place their charges and set timers. At the same time orders to abandon ship were given. Officers screamed out the order and it spread immediately to all hands.

"Abandon ship!"

"Abandon ship!"

Crewmen scrambled below decks to get through hatches as sea water surged past and explosions burst all over the ship knocking them from their feet. Pale-faced young men clambered up ladders, ran down companionways, shouting back to their comrades when they reached a dead end, flooded compartment, fire, gas, or a jammed hatch door.

Steffan left the engine room when an explosion demolished the propeller shaft and ruptured supply lines spewing oil throughout the compartment. He had been thrown onto his back and had heard a bone in his left arm crack as he landed near the hatch. He peered through the black smoke searching for signs of his comrades. He could see nothing, but he called out desperately. "I'm over by the hatchway door. Can you hear me? Alfred? Walter? Bruno?" Someone answered, coughing, choking, his voice shaky and strained. "Steffan? Yes, it is Alfred. I am coming...but I can't see. Keep talking and I will follow your voice." Steffan called out to Alfred guiding him through the compartment until he reached the hatch. "Anyone else?" Steffan called. "Can anyone else hear me?" He waited but there was no response. The two young men stared despairingly into the smoke as another blast erupted from deeper down and flames roared up into the chamber. They darted through the hatch, running, climbing, dodging bodies, maneuvering around twisted and jagged ruins of steel and a dangling maze of cables, joining others who were desperately seeking a way above decks, an escape route out of the dying ship.

This time I will catch the varmint. I just know it. The creature is gorging itself, scampering about from platter to platter, tasting and nibbling, climbing atop the food, its little feet pattering all over the special supper that had been laid out so nicely. It is completely engrossed in its feeding frenzy and totally unaware of me. I slink along the floor toward the counter. So slowly I move, hips down low to the ground. I know where I will jump up. There is a clear space just in front of where the rat is burrowing into a hunk of cheese. One spring up and I will be on it. One extension of my paw with claws extended and I will have it in my grasp. I get into position, loosening my hips with a brief wiggle and contracting my body as I hunch down ready for the leap.

It all happens in an instant. I jump up, burst into the air and land gracefully on the countertop. The rat's head darts up from the cheese and in a split second it sees me, spins and veers away. Its little legs hardly take a stride, though, before my paw shoots out and my claws sink into the soft flesh on the creature's back. I feel instant exhilaration and deep satisfaction as I tighten my paw, dragging the rat towards me for the kill. I have it! I've done it! The hunt is over! I have won!

It is at this moment. At the precise instant of my greatest victory when one of the enemy torpedoes tears through the side of the battleship amidships and explodes with a furor that brings my world crashing down. I am hurtled through the air turning end over end coming to an abrupt and painful stop when I smash against the wall of the compartment and drop to the floor. I lie there stunned and sore gasping for breath since the impact has knocked the air out of my lungs. My ears are ringing, and my eyes burn with dust and debris that has blown into them. Around me is total chaos. The compartment is littered with broken plates, dented and misshapen pots and pans, ruptured pipes hanging from overhead, food splattered everywhere, wires twisted and swaying with parts still attached and smoke belching up through holes in the floor. My first thought as my head clears is for Otto. Poor Otto! He will be devastated to see his kitchen like this. My next thought is for the rat. I glance down at *my paw. It is empty. Nothing is there. It has gotten away! Or has it? I jump to my feet and scan the room. The counter where I had been thrown from is squashed beneath a great steel beam and the food that had been on the countertop is splattered all about the room. The rat could be beneath the beam or amongst the twisted rubble around it. I tread carefully around the room searching amongst the debris of mangled kitchenware, shards of glass, hissing pipes, jagged pieces of broken crockery, but to no avail. The rat is nowhere to be found. Maybe it died in the explosion. Perhaps it fell through one of the gaping holes in the floor and into a fire below. It could have been thrown in the air as I had been and killed on impact somewhere in a wreckage-strewn corner. I will never know. I peer around me so deflated. I had held it in my grasp. I was but one second away from success, about to relish the sensation of my sharp teeth piercing the soft flesh on the back of the creature's neck as I clamped on in the inescapable death grip. But, I have been denied the ultimate victory and the satisfaction of the kill, my final moment of triumph and glory.*

***

Admiral Tovey aboard *King George V* watched through his binoculars as hit after hit tore apart the German warship. The British ships, *King George V*, *Rodney*, *Norfolk* and *Dorsetshire* fired from all sides reducing *Bismarck* to a floating, smoking, blazing wreck. There were men running about in desperation on the upper decks and superstructure, the once all-powerful gun barrels were destroyed and pointed every which way, there were holes and blown apart compartments down the entire length of the vessel. He saw that men were being thrown overboard with the blasts and some were jumping in voluntarily. It was obvious to all that *Bismarck* was doomed…and yet she was still afloat. In fact, Tovey saw that the foremast still stood and the bold, red ensign with the black crosses and swastika, was still flapping in the wind.

At 10:21 the British ships ceased firing. They were getting low on fuel and needed to return to base. Tovey ordered the *Dorsetshire,* the only ship with torpedoes remaining, to finish her off. *Dorsetshire* fired two torpedoes on the starboard side and at 10:36 one torpedo was fired on the port side. At 10:39 *Bismarck* sank.

Below decks while the final carnage was taking place,

the scenes of desperation, death and dying were dreadful. Hundreds of men were trapped in compartments where hatches were jammed shut or covered with heavy wreckage. Shell fire killed and injured men all over the ship. Flames cut off the whole forward part of the ship, men were trapped in a turret when the access hatch was jammed; blinding smoke caused men to fall through holes in the deck into raging fires below. Doctors and corpsmen were overwhelmed with casualties as more and more action stations were destroyed. Injured men needing immediate attention crowded the dressing stations as more were carried in on stretchers. All the while shells burst around them. Not much could be done under the circumstances. Morphine was given to relieve pain, but nothing could prevent the inevitable.

Steffan knew his time had come. A hatch was stuck. It would not budge even though strong, young seamen took turns pushing, prying and pounded on it with heavy iron rods. Seawater streamed into the compartment as explosions jarred and rocked the ship, knocking men off the ladder into the flood below. Steffan continued to scour the compartment for tools or a heavier staff to hand up to those struggling valiantly on the hatch, encouraging the effort, urging them on, but knowing it was useless. He knew they were doomed. Just before the torpedo hit that blew up the compartment and took all those young lives, Steffan thought of his family and home, his dear mother, Anna, his steady, hard-working father, Albert, Trina, his sweet-natured, lively little sister. He thought of Heidelberg, the river the hills…it was May…the hills would be covered with windflowers. A last thought was for Oscar. He wondered where he could be. The poor creature must be terrified, hiding in a remote corner somewhere. Poor Oscar, his faithful little friend. Steffan dearly wished that he could comfort the cat and that they could spend their last moments together.

CHAPTER TWELVE

ABANDON SHIP

I snapped out of my dejection and self-pity when I was unbalanced by another explosion. I knew that I had to move, leave the kitchen and get to the upper deck. I ran out of the compartment and into the open area beyond towards the ladders near the wardroom, but I stopped in my tracks before I got very far. I could not believe my eyes. It was total disaster. There was wreckage strewn everywhere and water was gushing in. To get to the ladders I would have to get my feet wet! I hate that. I considered the situation for a moment looking about me in all directions and then continued forward. I had to pick my way carefully through a mangle of metal and wires and cold seawater only to find that the ladders were twisted and buckled, and the hatches were closed. No one was about. All of the men had left the kitchen and wardroom during the night. I winced as an explosion close by above me caused dust and debris to rain down and I ran. I headed to the stern splashing through water, jumping over hunks of steel, dodging under pipes and beams lying at angles in my path. There were men further back in the ship. Men were climbing ladders, opening hatches, shouting out to each other and I headed for them and joined their ranks. They did not even notice me. All their attention and efforts were to move up, to find a way out. It was a maze, a dangerous game of trial and error, of dead ends and retracing steps to find an alternate route. I followed steadfastly, sprinting up ladders, racing down corridors, avoiding bodies and cringing with the loud blasts from the barrage of shells slamming into the ship. Smoke was everywhere and flames shot out from gaps and holes. More than once my paws were stepped on and I shrieked loudly in outrage, but no one heard or responded or cared.

***

Luckily the group that Oscar followed reached the main deck and dispersed in all directions, each man appraising the situation to determine when and where to abandon ship. Oscar took all of one second to decide that he would make for the stern on the starboard side where the smoke and fire seemed less intense. He clambered up to the upper deck and joined a group of men wearing life jackets as they stood waiting and listening to the direction of an officer. It was his friend, Mullenheim-Rechberg.

"There is still time. We're sinking slowly. The sea is running high, and we'll have to swim a long time, so it's best we jump as late as possible. I'll tell you when." The men nodded in response staring dolefully over the side at the surging sea.

"Don't worry," the officer continued. "Some ship will surely come along and pick us up." Oscar sat down in the middle of the group and waited there with them. He felt confident with this officer.

"Yes sir, Lieutenant, thank you sir," one of the sailors responded.

Two jolts in quick succession rocked the ship on the starboard side but not near Oscar's location on the upper deck. *Bismarck* was listing heavily to port, low in the water as waves broke over the main deck. And then enemy fire suddenly ceased. The guns had done their work. The last of the torpedoes would end it. *Dorsetshire* headed around to *Bismarck*'s port side and fired its last torpedo.

"It's that time!" cried Lieutenant Mullenheim-Rechberg. "Inflate your life jackets, prepare to jump."

The officer knew that the timing of abandoning the ship was crucial. It was important not to jump too early but it was also vital not to get sucked down by the sinking ship by delaying too long. Oscar stood up and paced restlessly. He knew what was about to happen. The men were going to jump over the side of the ship. But what about him! He had no life jacket. He could not swim. What was he to do? He peered into the churning ocean below him. The swells were frightening as they rose and fell rhythmically across the surface. He would not survive! But he would also die if he stayed aboard. It was a dilemma that no cat should have to endure.

"Oscar!" A voice called and a sailor crouched down beside him. Oscar gazed fondly into the kind and smiling face of Karl. "Oscar, look at you! Clever puss! I can't believe that you survived all this." The crewman scooped the cat up and held him in his arms. "Well, then you must come with us, my friend. We will jump together, eh, Oscar? We will jump together."

Lieutenant Mullenheim-Rechberg issued his last order. "A salute to our fallen comrades." The men glanced up at the flag, snapped their hands to their caps, and jumped. Karl held Oscar tightly as they fell but upon impact he lost his grip and the cat plunged down below the surface alone. The sudden, startling cold shocked him to the core. He tumbled deeper and deeper, twisting and turning in the water while scrabbling with his legs and paws to right himself. He had no idea how to function in water, but he instinctively strove toward the light. When he saw a geyser of bubbles bursting upward beside him, he followed them, and they seemed to speed him along until he finally broke the surface. There were men dotted all around him in the water calling to each other and swimming away from the sinking ship. Oscar followed their lead, his legs bicycling as hard as they could to push him forward. When they had reached a distance where they would be clear of suction when the ship went down, they stopped and turned to watch the last moments of the almighty *Bismarck*. Oscar was treading water desperately trying to stay with the men, but he was being drawn further and further away. He meowed but the sound was snatched by the wind and muffled by the waves. No one noticed him. The men were staring at the ship, now fully over on its side. Fires were squelched and smoke lessened as water jets hissed and shot high into the air through splits and holes in the hull and then with a pronounced gurgle, a death rattle, the mighty *Bismarck*, unsinkable ship of the German navy, slipped beneath the waves.

I have never felt so miserable in my life! Cold! I am so cold and wet. I am completely helpless out here. The waves are huge and strong, and I am being buffeted about and drawn away from my comrades. I cannot see Karl or Lieutenant Mullenheim-Rechberg. I have the most horrible taste in my mouth of salt and something worse which I think is the black, oily slick laying on top of the ocean. I cannot survive long like this; my strength will give out trying to keep my head above water, and the cold. How long can I endure it?

Something is floating in the water near me, rising and falling with the waves. It looks like the lid of one of the sea chests that I have seen in the storage compartments. Perhaps, if I try very hard and am lucky, I can make my way over to it.

***

The survivors in the Atlantic bobbed like corks trying to keep together in clusters as their life preservers kept them afloat and buoyant. They found themselves swept from group to group by the swell and pull of the waves. Lieutenant Mullenheim-Rechberg and Karl were among the men. Although he did not know it at the time, Lieutenant Mullenheim-Rechberg was the highest-ranking officer who had survived. Even from the surging seas of the cold Atlantic Ocean, he continued to lead doing his best to keep the men calm and calling out words of encouragement.

"Stay together! As soon as a ship comes, we'll swim over and get aboard." It was hard to stay optimistic, however. They were low in the water and could not see very far around them. When the swells lifted them higher, the men swiveled their heads around in all directions. Where were those British ships that had been shooting so aggressively at them? Surely they would come and pick up survivors. The cold was penetrating but the men were well dressed and were not yet feeling the effects too badly. The tension and emotion of the situation were uppermost in their minds. The stink of the oil which lay thickly and widely on the surface was sickening, as it blackened heads and faces while burning nostrils and throats as it forced its way into mouths, eyes, ears and noses. Some wreckage floated and rocked past as they drifted about but soon it was swept away. The men endured an hour or so of these helpless conditions, at the mercy of the tumultuous sea before, at the crest of the waves, they were finally able to spot a three-stack cruiser heading toward them.

"*Dorsetshire*!" Lieutenant Mullenheim-Rechberg called out. "Cheer up boys! We'll soon be aboard." The cruiser approached steadily closer and closer and then stopped before reaching the largest cluster of survivors. Men swam vigorously toward the ship and grasped at lines that were being thrown over the side. It was a desperate scene as weary sailors fought to reach the lines that were rising and falling with the roll of the ship and hold onto them in spite of the oil that now coated them. Some of the ropes had a bowline, a loop through which the men could shove a foot to be hoisted up by seamen above. Wooden rafts were lowered to provide respite and a means to catch breath for those waiting for their turn at the lines. Slowly men were being drawn out of the sea, hoisted up on their lines and pulled over the side by the outstretched hands of the enemy. *Dorsetshire* pulled 86 German sailors out of the Atlantic. Another British ship, the destroyer *Maori*, had also been ordered to pick up survivors and rescued 25 men.

Unfortunately, before the two ships finished the job, there was a submarine alert and they got underway immediately. They left the scene with hundreds of survivors still in the water, some still clinging to ropes along the ships' sides before they fell off. It was a horrific consequence of the tensions of a fierce war at sea that left those poor souls abandoned to a watery grave.

I was able to scramble on top of this crate lid, a small square of raft in the middle of this surging, rolling expanse of ocean. I drifted further and further away from my shipmates until I could no longer see any heads bobbing amongst the waves. I was desolate then. Alone, wet, cold and afraid. I lay down on the little raft digging my claws into the wood and mewing pitifully to myself as the uncaring sea bore me away.

I could not judge how much time passed because the sun was hidden behind a thick layer of clouds, but I floated helplessly for quite some time before I saw a shape far off on the horizon. I stared when I rose to the crest of the waves and could make out a mast and then a superstructure and then the bow of a ship fast approaching.

***

Aboard the British destroyer, *HMS Cossack*, Petty Officer Bowles was at his post on the bridge scanning the surface for periscopes as the ship maneuvered away from the recent battle zone and set its course to escort *King George V* to Loch Ewe on the Northwest coast of Scotland. The binoculars came to an abrupt halt as the Petty Officer suddenly caught sight of something floating in the water. He watched for a moment uncertain of what he saw and then he smiled in disbelief.

"Survivor in the water sir," he said. "Starboard side…100 meters…one o'clock, sir."

"Thank you, Bowles. Keep a look out for periscopes. We have no orders to recover survivors." Captain Vian responded in an authoritative monotone.

"No periscopes sighted on the starboard side, sir."

"No periscopes sighted on the port side, sir," added the lookout on the other side of the bridge.

"Er…sir…" continued Petty Officer Bowles, swallowing to prevent a laugh from erupting out of his throat, "it appears that the survivor is a cat, sir." The captain swung around to stare at the young man with a quizzical look.

"A what? *Cat*…did you say, Bowles?"

"Yes sir," he replied squinting through the binoculars, "a cat sitting on some wooden wreckage sir." Captain Vian strode over to Bowles and reached for the binoculars.

"Alright lad, let me take a look at this." He brought the binoculars up and scanned the waves until he saw the little raft with the miserable creature up on all fours staring back at him. "Bloody hell!" He exclaimed in amazement.

"Can we pick him up sir?"

"No, son," Vian replied regretfully. "We have our orders…"

"One attempt sir? I'll go over the side on a bowline. It will only delay us by five minutes sir."

Captain Vian hesitated. He was a dutiful officer who adhered steadfastly to regulation. He was disciplined and followed his orders to the letter. However, he had been deeply moved and shaken when the order was given to turn away from the German seamen still in the water. He followed orders but he silently grieved for those poor souls.

Petty Officer Bowles added one more plea. "Seems a shame sir…"

"Yes, it does! You have one attempt Bowles, just one."

"Yes *sir*!" The young man responded snapping a quick salute and spinning on his heels.

The ship steered toward the little raft and slowed engines. Bowles, with the help of a circle of men who soon realized that an unusual rescue was about to take place, was lowered over the side with his foot secure in a bowline. When he reached the surface, he saw that the raft was only a few meters away and he stretched one arm towards it while the other clung tightly to the line. He timed his lunge perfectly when the swell of a wave carried the raft closer. The Petty Officer grabbed the raft drawing it towards him and then he grasped the cat by the scruff of his neck. Oscar responded with an exhausted, sorrowful "*meow*." Bowles was hauled up and the survivor was welcomed aboard *HMS Cossack* by a growing group of men who stared in amazement and reached out to touch and comfort the pathetic little creature.

Oscar was toweled dry, fed, and given a coarse, folded blanket to rest on. He lay there in a corner of the wardroom (a lot smaller than the one on Bismarck but otherwise much the same) where some of the crew were off duty reclining in hammocks or talking in groups. From time to time a crewman wandered over and gave Oscar a little pet and scratch. Their speech was so different from the German to which he was accustomed. He did not understand any of their words, but he could grasp their meaning from the tone of voice and the compassion and friendliness with which they were spoken. They were the enemy, Oscar knew. The British. But they did not seem so very different, just other young men, aboard another ship, doing their jobs. Not very different at all. When he was stronger and more inclined, he would learn some of the language and interact with these young sailors. Now, though, as Oscar warmed, and relaxed and dozed, his thoughts were on his friends of the *Bismarck*.

Oh, how I grieve! What has become of the courageous crew? How many of the young men from the wardroom have survived? I saw so many bodies and so many injured and dying during that last battle. What about Conrad, my red-headed friend from provisions who stocked the pantries? I hope he made it out! I thought I glimpsed Captain Lindemann at the end. There was a figure that looked like him climbing the steep angle of the bow gazing up at the flag on the mast and pausing to salute just before the ship rolled over and went down. Otto, good-hearted, Otto, who took such care to make sure that I was well-fed, is he somewhere out there in the ocean, abandoned and left to die? Who will call me his little miezekatze now? And Steffan, my dear friend; he cared for me, consoled me and kept me close all those months that we were on board together. He took me home... I don't think he made it up from the engine room. I do hope that Karl made it. He saved me by carrying me with him overboard. I don't think I would have been able to make that jump by myself.

We did not believe that Bismarck could ever sink but here I am, a survivor...a prisoner of war. What will become of me now? At the moment, I really do not care. I am tired, indifferent and so very sad. As my eyes close, a last thought of the rat. It got away from me, escaped from my clutches, but only because of the torpedo blast and shelling. It must be dead now also, lying at the bottom of the sea. I suppose I am the winner after all. And with that satisfying thought, I fall into a deep, dreamless sleep.

EPILOGUE

Slowly, Oscar recovered from the trauma of his last hours aboard *Bismarck* and he came to know some of the men aboard this new ship, *Cossack*. Always needful of performing a purposeful task, he took to his mouser activities, scouting out the location of the kitchen and food storage compartments. Since the ship was so much smaller than *Bismarck* had been, he was able to keep a closer eye on mouse activity. He quickly caught two young mice and left them in the wardroom so that his new shipmates would know that he was on duty. He was treated well, gaining the affection and respect of the men and, in a remarkable coincidence, *was named Oscar by the British crew!*

HMS Cossack escorted *King George V* to Loch Ewe after the sinking of *Bismarck* and then continued on to Scapa Flow. During the next few months, the destroyer performed escort duties in the Northwest Passage, to Gibraltar, and in the Mediterranean Sea. On October 23, 1941, only five months after Oscar was rescued from the ocean, a torpedo from a German U-boat blew up the fore part of the ship killing the captain and 158 crew outright.

The survivors abandoned ship, most floating in or hanging onto Carley Floats (oval-shaped floats of cork and canvas with a wooden or webbed floor.) Oscar was tossed into one of the floats suddenly and hastily by a well-meaning sailor and he found himself wet again, floundering in swishing water at the bottom of the float. Soon, though the men on his raft were taken aboard another destroyer *HMS Legion* and were brought to Gibraltar, a British port which controlled the passage of ships between the Atlantic Ocean and the Mediterranean Sea.

In Gibraltar, the cat earned the name "Unsinkable Sam" when knowledge of his two survival events spread and he was rewarded with a transfer to *HMS Ark Royal*, a distinguished British aircraft carrier. This was a very different experience for Oscar. The ship carried planes and he watched with awe as they roared off of the deck into the sky and returned with skids and the catch of a hook. *Ark Royal* was ferrying planes to Malta, an island in the Mediterranean besieged by the enemy, and Oscar had only been on board for a couple of weeks when it too was torpedoed. Fortunately, the aircraft carrier sank very slowly and there was only one fatality. The crew was removed to rescue ships while a select damage control party stayed aboard in an attempt to save the ship. (This party was later removed when efforts proved unsuccessful and *Ark Royal* was towed to Gibraltar for repairs but sunk en route, 30 miles away.) Oscar had somehow ended up *again* in the water and was found by a motor launch clinging to a wooden plank. He was pulled once more from the water, this time hissing and angry with no intention of displaying any sign of his usual dignity and reserve.

The incensed cat was transferred to *HMS Legion* (the same ship that had rescued him from *Cossack*) and taken to Gibraltar again with other survivors. There he was considered to be "unlucky" and was assigned to land duty in the offices of the Governor. He wandered around the offices of Government House, appreciative at first of the respite from dangers at sea but feeling out of his element and of little use. The kitchen was impeccably clean and orderly, and he never found a sign of any varmints there. He contented himself with hunting in the gardens and grounds surrounding the building and lying in the warm sunshine.

The following spring a brave ship took Oscar aboard

and sailed (uneventfully) from Gibraltar to Belfast, Ireland where he was placed in a sailors' home. The old but noble brick building was located on the docks of the city and Oscar felt immediately at home. He could walk down to the busy wharves and watch the bustle of activity which reminded him so much of the docks at Hamburg where his life at sea had begun. It was exciting watching ships of all sorts and sizes tying up and unloading their cargos while eager young men disembarked with duffel bags slung over their shoulders looking for a place to stay, a hot meal and a pretty girl. He was content living in the sailors' home where men of the sea, young and old, found a comfortable repose and safe place to stay while in port. The home inside somewhat resembled the galleys and cabins aboard ship and the decorations were salty, rustic and familiar. Oscar was gratified to have purpose there and was much appreciated by the residents since mice from the docks would often find their way into the building.

And so, the scent of sea air continued to drift in with the wind and Oscar was happy although he often watched the port from an elevated perch and stared out beyond Belfast Lough to the horizon, to the sea. He would think of them then, the seamen he had known, men of the mighty warship *Bismarck*, pride of the Kriegsmarine.

***

The survivors of Bismarck on board *Dorsetshire* were taken to Newcastle, England and survivors from *Maori* were landed at a base on the river Clyde, Scotland. All were taken to London for interrogation before spending the rest of the war in prisoner of war camps. Three more survivors were picked up by a U-boat during the evening of May 27th and two by the German weather ship, *Sachsenwald*, the next day.

AUTHOR'S NOTE

It is a fact that mascots have been part of voyages at sea during peacetime and wartime since man first hoisted sail. They have been utilized for the purpose of boosting morale amongst the crew by providing a common bond, for stress relief and comfort and, in the case of a cat, keeping down the all-too-common infestation of rats and mice.

When I first discovered the legend of Oscar and became familiar with the dramatic events of the ill-fated *Bismarck*, I thought it would be interesting to tell the story of the battleship including the activities and thoughts of its little mascot.

There are several reports of Oscar, and a portrait of the cat is included in the collection of the National Maritime Museum in Greenwich, England. There are also however, accounts of denials of members of the crews of the ships in which Oscar allegedly sailed, that a cat was ever aboard. Therefore, it is up to the reader to decide. I choose to believe that he did indeed exist and used up several of his lives during his time at sea.

The events of the battles at sea are described as

they happened and I have used as my main resource a book written by Kapitanleutnant Mullenheim-Rechburg, *Bismarck: A Survivor's Story*. Kapitanleutnant Mullenheim-Rechburg was an officer and the most senior surviving member of the crew. Although his interactions with Oscar are fictionalized, he was indeed a skilled artillery officer. The events of the rescue by Cossack were taken from his own account and I have quoted him from his book almost exactly. I came to respect and admire the officer very much as I read his book. He recognized the flaws in decisions made by Lutjens and the contentious relationship between Lutjens and Lindemann, but he did not for a moment let his doubts known or react in any negative way. He fought bravely and performed his duties until the end and even in the water he continued to lift the spirits of the men. He respected the enemy and remained friends with many of his British counterparts following his years as a prisoner of war.

FEATURED SHIPS

Activities and fate of ships in the story following the sinking of Bismarck

HMS ARK ROYAL British aircraft carrier - 1937 – 1941

Involved in supporting convoys to Malta

Torpedoed in 1941 by a German U-boat resulting in one fatality

Sunk 30 miles from Gibraltar

HMS AURORA British light cruiser – 1936 – mid 1950s

Involved in activities off the coast of Norway, the Mediterranean, North Africa, Sicily and the 1944 landings in south France

Sold in 1948 to the Chinese navy and renamed *Chung King*, crew defected to the Communists in 1949, ship sunk one month later by Nationalists, ship salvaged and became a warehouse ship

BISMARCK German battleship – 1939 -1941

Conducted extensive sea trials in the Baltic Sea 1939-

1940

Destroyed *HMS Hood* in the Atlantic – May 1941
Pursued by dozens of British warships and was disabled by a torpedo hit to her rudder dropped by a Swordfish plane
Damaged by fierce bombardment of British ships and sunk on May 27, 1941

HMS COSSACK British destroyer - 1937 – 1941
Involved in escort activities in the Northwest Passage and the Mediterranean between Gibraltar and Malta
Hit by a torpedo in October 1941 while escorting a convoy from Gibraltar to U.K. killing 159 but stays afloat
Ship sank in Atlantic while under tow.

HMS DORSETSHIRE British Heavy Cruiser – 1929 - 1942
Provided cover for convoy from Canada to India
Sunk in Indian Ocean 1942 by Japanese dive bombers, 234 killed

HMS GALATEA British light cruiser – 1934 – 1941
Involved in escort activities in the Mediterranean, off

coast of Malta and North Africa

Torpedoed and sunk by German U-boat December 1941, 470 killed

HMS HERMIONE British light cruiser – 1939 – 1942

Involved in escort activities in the Mediterranean

Torpedoed while escorting a supply convoy from Alexandria to Malta June 1942, 87 killed

HMS HOOD British battle cruiser – 1920 – 1941

World's largest warship for two decades

Sunk by Bismarck in the Denmark Strait on May 24, 1941

1,415 men killed, 3 survivors

HMS KENYA British destroyer – 1939 – 1962

Intercepted U-boats escorting enemy ships to the Atlantic

Involved in escort activities for convoys to Malta

Involved in escorting Arctic convoy

Scrapped in 1962

HMS KING GEORGE V British battleship – 1939 – 1957

Supported allied landings in Sicily – 1943

Involved in bombarding Japanese installations in the Pacific

Flagship of the British Home Fleet

Scrapped in 1957

HMS LEGION British destroyer – 1939 – 1942

Involved in escort activities for convoys to Malta

Involved in enemy air attack on Malta

Sank in harbor in 1942

HMS MAORI British destroyer – 1937 – 1942

Involved in Battle of Cape Bon off the coast of Tunisia December 1941

Sank off coast of Malta in 1942 by German aircraft, 1 dead

HMS NEPTUNE British light cruiser – 1933 – 1941

Intercepted convoy bound for Tripoli – 1941

Struck 4 mines, sank, 767 killed, 1 survivor

HMS NORFOLK British heavy cruiser – 1928 – 1950

Involved in escorting Arctic convoys to and from Russia

Hit while involved in sinking German ship *Scharnhorst*

Sold for scrap in 1950

ORP PIORUN Polish destroyer – 1940 – 1955

Involved in activities in the Mediterranean escorting convoys to Malta

Involved in activities off the coast of Sicily

Scrapped in 1955

HMS PRINCE OF WALES British Battleship – 1941 – 1941

Damaged in action with *Bismarck*

Carried Churchill in August to meet FDR for Atlantic Charter Conference

Involved in activities in the Mediterranean

Sunk in December by bombing and torpedoes from Japanese planes while countering the Japanese threat in the Far East

PRINZ EUGEN German heavy cruiser – 1938 – 1946

Torpedoed by British submarine in 1942

Under repair, 1943

Bombarded Baltic coast against Soviets, 1944-45

Surrendered to British May 1945

Americans used ship for nuclear test in 1946 at Bikini Atoll

Capsized in December 1946

HMS RENOWN British battle cruiser – 1916 -1948

Involved in Arctic convoy activity

Transported Churchill to various conferences

Involved in the Indian Ocean in 1944 bombarding Japanese installations in Indonesia

Scrapped in 1948

HMS REPULSE British battle cruiser – 1916 – 1941

Sunk by the Japanese with *Prince of Wales* in the Far East

HMS RODNEY British battleship – 1925 – 1948

Involved in activities in the Mediterranean, Gibraltar, Malta Iceland, North Africa, Sicily and supported the Normandy Invasion in 1944

Escorted the Murmansk convoy

Scrapped in 1948

SACHSENWALD German weather ship – 1939 – 1944

Picked up two survivors in a raft from sunk German battleship, *Bismarck,* May 28, 1941

Transitioned to a patrol boat and was sunk by British ships while transporting ammunition along French coast from St. Nazaire to La Pallice

HMS SHEFFIELD British Cruiser – 1936 – 1967

Involved in Arctic convoy activity

Involved in activities in North Africa, the Barents Sea, the Bay of Biscay and Salerno

Involved in the sinking of German battle cruiser, *Scharnhorst* in 1943

After World War II involved in activities in the West Indies and the Mediterranean

Scrapped in 1967

HMS SIKH British destroyer – 1937-1942

Involved in activities in the Mediterranean where she sank a German submarine

Sunk off the coast of Tobruk by German anti-aircraft batteries, 115 men lost

HMS SUFFOLK British heavy cruiser – 1926 – 1948

Involved in Arctic convoy activity until 1942

Underwent a refit until 1943

Involved in operation in the Indian Ocean for the remainder of the war

Scrapped in 1948

HMS VICTORIOUS British aircraft carrier – 1939 – 1968

Involved in Arctic convoy operations to Soviet Union

Provided air cover for operations in Malta and North Africa

Loaned to U.S. in 1943

Underwent refit and renamed *USS Robin*

Involved in action in the Pacific Ocean

Returned to British

Involved in bombardment operations in the Far East and Okinawa in 1945

Utilized for training activities after 1948

Refit and utilized by the Home Fleet until 1968

Scrapped in 1968

HMS ZULU British destroyer – 1937 – 1942

Involved in the bombardment of Tobruk, Libya in 1942

Sunk by Italian fighter-bombers in 1942

39 men killed

ABOUT THE AUTHOR

England was Frances' childhood home. She emigrated to the United States with her family as a teenager many years ago. Although she loves America, a part of her heart always remains in the country of her birth.

Frances has been a storyteller for as long as she can remember with her first audience consisting of neighborhood playmates sitting on the curb listening to her tall tales. More recently, she has written and told or performed her nautical themed stories for school children visiting on field trips at a local seaport association where she worked.

She has visited numerous organizations, upon request, to speak about *The Forgotten Flag*, her first published work, and continues to visit classrooms at local schools to meet students who have read the book as part of their American History curriculum.

Frances worked for many years at a high school in Connecticut in the English and Social Studies

Departments which provided the perfect environment to inspire her love of history and writing. She has self-published several books, *The Brass Bell, The Curse of the Shark's Tooth*, and *Oscar of the Bismarck* which are young adult stories, as well as *St. Katherine's Dock*: *Target Tower Bridge* adult historical fiction. While working at the school, she prepared presentations for teachers to enhance their curriculum and subject matter when it pertained to British history. These have included the Elizabethan Era to better understand the time of Shakespeare, the Victorian Era to portray the time of Charles Dickens, and World War II – the British Homefront.

When her mother passed away several years ago, Frances decided that her story must be told. *Vera's Story: Hidden Scars of War* tells the tale of a not so ordinary, woman whose memories of war were never far below the surface.

https://www.francesyevan.com